LIBERATION SAGA

VOLUME 1

F. LOCKHAVEN
M.A. OWENS

TWISTED KEY
p u b l i s h i n g
2024

First Printing: 2024

ISBN 978-1-63911-136-7

Twisted Key Publishing, LLC
www.twistedkeypublishing.com

Ordering Information:
Special discounts are available on quantity purchases by corporations, associations, educators, and others. For details, contact the publisher at the above listed address.

U.S. trade bookstores and wholesalers: Please contact Twisted Key Publishing, LLC by email twistedkeypublishing@gmail.com.

TABLE OF CONTENTS

Prologue 1
Chapter 1 12
Chapter 2 25
Chapter 3 33
Chapter 4 42
Chapter 5 49
Chapter 6 57
Chapter 7 65
Chapter 8 73
Chapter 9 82
Chapter 10 90
Chapter 11 99
Chapter 12 108
Chapter 13 116
Chapter 14 124
Chapter 15 132
Chapter 16 140
Chapter 17 148
Chapter 18 158
Chapter 19 166
Chapter 20 174
Frelya: Hopes and Dreams 182

Prologue

Ghost and I sat quietly, watching the scene in front of us. A distraction no one asked for. Vibrant vegetation, kissed by the sun, swaying in a gentle wind, failed to warn anyone of what awaited them if they looked over their shoulder.

Chaos. Destruction. Disappointment. The death of dreams. The pinnacle and the end of humanity.

The walls of PanTech HQ crumbled in many places, far into the distance. It was too dangerous to approach now. Machines still patrolled the interior, shaped like spiders and as big as a house. Thankfully, they had not emerged from within. At least not yet. My small crew of Explorers League stragglers barely escaped a pursuit party filled with them, but it wasn't without cost. Everyone still inside was likely lost. Many had been lost on the outside.

I stole a quick look at myself in a small pocket mirror I carried, half-expecting to see gray hairs and wrinkles. Yet, somehow, I still looked like a young woman in her early twenties. Seeing myself, I couldn't help but think of my mother. My raven hair and dark, narrow eyes were just like hers. Inheriting my father's darker skin was the only thing that set me apart from a younger her.

I missed them so much…

"I'll catch up in a bit, Ghost. Could you work with Linda on stocking our vehicle for the journey?"

"There's one more matter I'd like to discuss first," he said.

"Oh? Very serious. What is it, Ghost?"

"I believe we should visit your home zone first."

"Ghost… you know how badly I want to do that, but that's not the plan. Arc City has the highest population of any zone. It must be prioritized to prevent the most deaths. Going to any other zone first would be impractical. I understand you're saying it for my sake, but we cannot deviate from this."

"For your sake? Do you think I'm a human, weighed down by your same erratic emotions? Please… It's just that, as usual, you are failing to factor in all variables and, therefore, are arriving at the wrong conclusion."

"Please, Ghost," I said, slamming down my pen and paper beside me. "I'm all ears. Go on. Tell me why I'm wrong."

"This mission requires you to be at your very best to stand any chance. Even then, it's impossible. You will always be distracted by thoughts of home. Every time you see a woman dying, you'll think of your mother. When you see a man, you'll think of your father. Traveling to your zone first will eliminate these distractions and allow you to enter Arc City at your very best, significantly increasing the chances of a positive outcome."

"I..." I wanted to argue. I balled up my fist, letting my mind fill with the various ways I was about to tell Ghost he was wrong. Except he wasn't. It was already becoming what I thought about the most. What if Ferris went home, expecting I would too? "Okay..." I said, almost whispering. "We'll go there first."

"I'll leave you to your letter," Ghost said, taking off and flying toward the survivor camp.

Ghost might not have understood humans very well in general, but he certainly understood me. He questioned the usefulness of penning such a letter, leaving it for someone to find, sealed in a container to be found someday in the future. But... I just wanted to believe there would be a future. If not for us, then for someone. The anthropomorphic animals we created, perhaps. Maybe by some miracle humans really would survive. I wanted to believe someone might find it... even though, deep in my heart, this letter was, in truth, only for me. I doubted anyone would ever find it.

I took a deep breath, sighed, and began writing.

Hello, stranger.

My name is Taylor.

I'm writing this letter because tomorrow I depart to "save" what remains of humanity.

I was born in a small village. An adversity zone isolated in the vast desert. My mother was a PanTech sympathizer and former employee. My mother was practical and resourceful. When she put her mind to it, there was almost nothing she couldn't do.

My father was a stubborn man. A genius and an inventor. More than that, he had a rebellious heart. One he passed on to me. He believed forcing others was always wrong, even when they were forced to do good.

When I was nearly eighteen, just before I was meant to take the PanTech employee entrance exam all young people of every zone take after their eighteenth birthday, my life took a sharp turn. As my village's veterinarian, I was the first to notice when a strange new species, more monster than animal, began attacking.

Surprisingly, or I guess unsurprisingly in hindsight, this was a PanTech engineered weapon meant to bring our village's progress down a notch. To put us in our place. With the help of a PanTech soldier named Linus, willing to stand up against his own employer to do what he felt was right, the two of us challenged the monster in the desert. Afterward, Linus was killed by fellow soldiers. He was the first man I truly loved.

Shortly after this, I met the creature who would become my dearest non-human friend. Little is known about shadowfalcons, beyond the fact they were thought to be a made-up species. Just in case this letter was to ever fall into the wrong hands, I'll not get into the specifics of what makes them special. Shadowfalcons are equipped with the ability to disable prey easily, but more than that, they possess the highest intellect of any animal I'm aware of. When he was later used as a prototype for a humanization study, this increased notably. I'll get more into that later.

I confronted the commander in charge of my zone, a fiery woman named Frelya. I felt she was partially responsible for what happened to Linus. I thought she ordered it. Turned out, she didn't. Knowing her the way I came to know her later, it hurts my heart to write anything mean about her. Just know that, at that time, I hated her. I thought she was a shining example of everything I loathed about PanTech and the world.

I made some efforts to join a rebel group in the village, but found they were no better than those we stood against. Worse, they'd set Linus up and were the reason he was killed. I could never forgive them. I confronted them, eventually leading to a show-down with the leader. I walked away. He didn't. Because of this, I was given special recognition by PanTech recruiters for squashing a rebellion, even though that was never my intention. My brother and I passed our exams and were shipped off shortly after. With Frelya pulling some strings, I was implanted with an enhancer, as we call them. A small device in the brain that allows us to push our bodies and minds beyond the limits of what we thought possible. Normally, only given to commanders.

I haven't seen my brother Ferris since the collapse, but I don't think he was here when it happened. I hope he's okay...

After arriving at PanTech, adjusting was easier than I expected. I met two wonderful friends, Linda and Joyce. They were by my side, always, and they taught me the valuable life lesson of how to depend on others, to lean on friends in times when the world felt too overwhelming. I knew that, no matter what I faced, I could always count on them.

And I'd face a lot after joining PanTech.

Shortly after I joined—in the Animal Studies division—we worked on the first test subjects for our animal humanization project. We gave them more human features, a higher intellect, the ability to speak and use tools. Our first experiment was on a Beagle, which we named Henry. An adorable little guy. This science was secretly planned for military use, of course, by the president's confidant, General Markus. The same man who would betray him and attempt to establish a military dictatorship. Thankfully, with the help of Frelya, Linda, and Joyce, we were able to stop him. I overused my enhancer in this fight, nearly dying, prompting Frelya to remove it and install a weaker, but much safer version.

I never thought I'd say this but... perhaps we shouldn't have stopped the general.

After the fiasco with the general, leader of Adversity Management, I was allowed to take half of the newly created anthropomorphic dogs and cats back with me to form a new division called the Explorers League. We specialized in exploring old territories and discovering their historical significance lost to time. However, we found that the more we explored, the more we encountered these strange old-world machines. Arachnids. Giant spider machines. At first, they were all rust buckets barely posing any threat, but my units learned how to fight them, disable them, and exploit their weaknesses. Something that would make all the difference later.

It was only after removing Markus as a threat that I began to realize what a madman the president of PanTech truly was. Like a villain in a story, he sought endless strength and immortality. He dreamed of reshaping humanity in his own image. No price was too high for even the most trivial of his goals. And that being the case, the development of a supervirus had been going on in secret. One he hoped could be programmed to weed out the less intellectually gifted, distilling humanity down to a few hundred immortal geniuses with no need to consider population.

When I opposed this, I was "reeducated," which is a process too horrific to describe in detail. It was like a different version of me was installed in my body and able to make all the decisions. It controlled my logic. It made me... a horrible person. I'd met a man right before this, named Farle, and I thought I might have finally found someone. That I was finally able to move on. The new me ruined everything, got his sister killed, and led him to resent everyone. Myself, PanTech, and the world. It was then that, in truth, I probably had the most in common with him.

Frelya was the one who freed me from the nightmare, though I only wish she'd managed to do it sooner. A feat no one had ever been able to perform, she reversed the reeducation procedure. Even the president couldn't believe it, making it easy for me to conceal that I'd been made myself again. We attempted to stop him from moving forward with the virus, but all this failed. He eliminated anyone who stood against him and proved to be unbeatable. Though not unstoppable.

A cat named Kelin intervened to stop Farle from killing me. This same cat was how we discovered the president's secret immortality experiments. They'd been disguised within our animal studies. It was only when we began to inspect their changed DNA that we realized it. Harlow, a dog who was Kelin's rival in the beginning, became her great friend. When she was captured, he risked his life to rescue her. Kelin might've saved me from Farle, but Harlow wasn't to be outdone.

Frelya and I confronted the president together, hoping to stop the inevitable but... we failed. Seeing that we couldn't win, Frelya forced me to eject from the building through its elevator. Harlow and Kelin picked me up afterward, and we began our escape. Followed by a swarm of these freshly assembled arachnid machines, my Explorers League protected me. Harlow sacrificed himself to disable our pursuers with an EMP, allowing the others a precious window of time to destroy them. By a hair, we escaped.

I should not be here right now, alive, writing this letter. During the collapse, before he was killed, Farle schemed to infect the animals in both Adversity Management and Explorers League, sending them out to every zone to infect all humanity. He destroyed our long-range communication systems to prevent us from sending out any kind of warning. There was no stopping it. Now, all I have is the version of the vaccine we were able to create before our science facilities were destroyed. A false salvation. Protection from the virus at the cost of fertility. Life, in exchange for complete sterilization.

Humanity is finished, but I'm compelled to give everyone who remains the choice. If one day, humans find this, I want to apologize to you for the role I played in all this. I'm sorry I wasn't enough to save you. I wish I could have done better. Offered more. Been more. If animals can outlive us all, and one finds this in the distant future, I can only ask you for this one favor:

Don't repeat our mistakes. Learn to see the value in others and treasure their differences. Appreciate those who disagree with you the most, because it is them who make you better than who you were yesterday. Your rivals encourage you to rise above your previous limits. Love them for that.

Don't strive to be the next humanity.

Be better.

I folded the letter and locked it in the canister, sealing it tightly. I'd written it more for myself than for others, knowing it was unlikely anyone would ever see it.

I turned around, getting on my knees and crawling beneath the overhang of the large boulder I'd been sitting on, digging away with my bare hands to create a shallow hiding place.

It was a weight off my shoulders. A weight I was about to replace with one a hundred times heavier.

I was finally ready to take my next step forward.

Chapter 1

This homecoming would be a challenging one. Not only because it had been a few years since I last spoke to my parents, but because the entire world changed in that time. I went from a poor villager who had never even seen electricity to an elite PanTech employee, creating genetically modified anthropomorphic animals in the most scientifically advanced laboratories humanity had ever conceived. That not being enough, I became the youngest professor the organization ever promoted... shortly before playing an active role in destroying it. I was little better than an outlaw now. Not that PanTech was in any position to collect on a bounty. The horrific situation they'd created by failing to contain a deadly virus of their own making was far worse than any offense I could've ever committed. My only true crime was trying to stop them.

And failing. Perhaps *that*, failing, was my true crime.

"Are you sure leaving the lab so far away from our destination is the wisest decision?" Ghost asked, preening his feathers.

I sighed, cursing under my breath as my hand slipped off one of the delicate wires I was trying, with great difficulty, to replace under the seat of my motorcycle.

"Am I sure? With everything that's happened in the past few weeks, I don't know if there's a single thing I'm sure of. I know you're worried, Ghost, but I can't risk anyone else getting their hands on my laboratory vehicle. They do that, and we're finished. No more vaccine. No more mission."

Ghost stared blankly, tilting his head a bit at my comment. A falcon staring blankly was the default, after all. Their faces didn't exactly allow for much emotion.

"The same could be said for you. No more Taylor, no more mission."

I snapped the seat back down on the bike with an unnecessary amount of force.

"If there was a way to get back into PanTech HQ and reestablish global communication, that wouldn't need to be the case. Being able to coordinate with all the adversity zones would… well we wouldn't be in this mess right now if we could do that. That system was completely decimated by the battle, and there's no way to get back in there even if there was something we could do to restore it."

"There's no accounting for things that can't be. Your focus is better spent elsewhere," Ghost said in his usual stoic, matter-of-fact way.

"Thanks for the pep talk, Ghost. Hearing that frustrates me, but you're right of course. We must work with what we have... which is why I'm not bringing this lab anywhere near remnants of PanTech's Adversity Management. It can stay cloaked in that ravine for months if it needs to."

Ghost nodded several times, with a hint of enthusiasm.

"Understood."

Adversity Management... PanTech's great experiment without a conclusion. Place a group of humans within the confines of a challenging environment and monitor how this affects the kind of person they become. Some very primitive, not unlike humanity's original cavemen. One, I'd heard, was filled with bustling neon streets based on the early twentieth century. Gangsters and police grappling for control. My own village, a group of desert dwellers, few in number, making their way in life with little more than basic tools and the clothes on their backs. Yet PanTech's demise was in truth brought about by a solitary ambitious tyrant, and the only man at PanTech who had never stepped foot in an adversity zone. Its own president, seeking immortality and dooming humanity in the process. All other employees were recruited based on test scores, on a test administered to all citizens of every adversity zone after reaching the age of eighteen.

Strength Through Adversity! This was their slogan. Shouted at the conclusion of every meeting. Proudly proclaimed before every salute. The justification given to excuse every atrocity those hypocrites committed. I sighed, returning my focus to the task at hand. Now wasn't the time to get absorbed in my rage. Again.

"Time to test the barrier," I said, rising to my feet and taking a few steps forward.

Placing my hand in front of me, I winced, forcing another step before giving up and stumbling back.

"They've altered the barrier?" Ghost asked.

"They have. Probably before communication was severed with HQ. I'll need to get an encryption key to fully eliminate the problem but that'll require making contact with a Pan-Tech Adversity Management soldier. We both know what a mixed bag that is. I'm going to guess their last intel was to never let me or any of the other defectors anywhere near an adversity zone."

I spat, kicking sand toward the barrier. I'd gotten better at managing my frustration, but that frustration was building.

I had a limited amount of time to "save" as much of humanity as possible from the virus, using a cure that wasn't much better. By now, it was likely everyone was already infected. Pan-Tech, and Farle, made absolutely sure of that.

"I'll fly over and see if I can detect any weak points," Ghost finally said, allowing me a moment to contemplate before acting on his own.

"Thank you, Ghost. Be careful. They may try to shoot you down. Even with cloaking, you can still be spotted with the human eye."

"You should be careful too, Taylor. You'll be easier to shoot than me."

I grinned. "I always appreciate your humor, Ghost, and the fact that I'm never sure whether it's humor."

Ghost flew off without clarifying.

He was right, either way. To appear as little of a threat as possible, I'd opted to take only my sword, Twisted Key, and a small sidearm as weapons—my PanTech employee uniform with Frelya's ingenious armor beneath. That loadout, combined with the enhancer embedded in my brain, meant I'd easily outmatch anyone below the rank of commander. I just wouldn't look it.

The enhancer was one of the few things I was thankful for from my time at PanTech. A brain implant that enhanced my mental and physical capabilities—conveniently hidden within the walls of my own skull—was sure to come in handy.

Still, a surprise direct hit from a standard-issue PanTech rifle would kill me instantly, even if a child fired it.

The image flooded back into my mind again. Frelya, standing above me with crimson curls blowing in the wind, her hand on the elevator switch. We were meant to fight together. She was invincible. PanTech's model warrior.

It had been weeks, and Frelya hadn't been spotted. She never escaped, and all attempts to organize rescues of the hundreds still trapped inside failed against a growing number of machines amassing within PanTech's walls. As if I needed more problems. It seemed almost inevitable these mechanical demons would eventually leave the walls and… who could say after that? One problem at a time. The virus was more pressing. The virus came first. One adversity zone, then another, and another.

After rolling the bike behind a rock, I started walking, taking only essential supplies in my pack. This was one of the smallest adversity zones under PanTech control, and I could circle the entire perimeter in just a few days if I needed to. This was my homeland. I knew the terrain, what was safe to eat and what wasn't, which animals were dangerous, and so on.

However, walking alone with only my thoughts to keep me company was perhaps the worst thing for me to experience now. After our daring escape from PanTech's collapse, fighting off dozens of massive machines, losing friends… not knowing if some were lost or only missing. The chaos of this new world was almost too much to bear, and yet I had to bear it. Including some of the responsibility for the virus itself.

After all, if I'd closed off my heart just a little tighter, Farle wouldn't have been able to use me to gain access to the virus, to intentionally contract it himself, to spread it to the anthropomorphic dogs and cats to act as silent carriers, send them to every adversity zone, then destroy their communication so no one could warn them away. The perfect storm of impossible problems with even more impossible solutions.

I clenched my teeth and shook my head violently, willing myself back to reality. Back to the present. Ghost was right. What's done is done.

Just as my focus returned, I spotted a two-person patrol in the distance. Inside their suits it was hard to tell the difference between human and animal soldier, but the fact they were in one of these white power suits meant they were part of Adversity Management. They likely wouldn't take kindly to my arrival. However…

"Hello there!" I shouted, waving and smiling. "I'm lost. Can you help a girl out?"

Immediately, their attention snapped to me.

"Identify yourself!" one shouted.

"Now!" said the other, not even giving me the time to follow the command.

"Professor Taylor of the Explorers League. I'm not lost, obviously, but it seems I can't get in with my previous clearance. Help a girl out?"

They weren't going to help me out, and I knew that. At least not willingly. Especially now that their voices identified them as distinctively human. I certainly didn't know many humans in Adversity Management who would take my side in all this, given the list of charges I was likely facing. Sedition, attempted murder of PanTech's president, stolen property, conspiracy... likely only limited by human creativity. Successful murder of PanTech's president would've been a better one. I could only hope my friend Frelya managed to finish that job.

"Stay right there. Do not move," the first voice called out again. Less aggression. Anxiety and uncertainty in his tone. Fear, perhaps. I wished I could see their faces.

They passed through the barrier. That was step one. Step two wasn't going to be as easy as the first.

"Hands where I can see them," ordered the second soldier.

I raised my hands in the air slowly. Very slowly. If they were attempting to approach me with just the two of them, it meant their communication was unreliable as well. If their intel had been complete and accurate, they'd know better.

One kept their sidearm pointed at me from a short distance away while the other took hold of my wrists.

"For now, we'll be taking you into custody," he said.

"Sorry," I replied, my voice filled with authentic pity.

With a quick burst of strength, I overpowered the much bigger man holding my wrists, despite the fact his strength was greatly amplified by his suit. Surprised, he did little to counter. As the other soldier readied his sidearm to fire, I moved the first soldier between us, kicking him in the chest and sending him flying into the other, knocking them both to the ground.

They struggled to their feet, but I was on them in the blink of an eye, ripping the helmet from the first soldier and delivering a punch that sent him to the ground again, unconscious. The second soldier fell on his back, panicked, bringing up his sidearm. Not good. I could easily sidestep the trajectory, but the sound might alert others and if others meant a commander...

Before the blaster could be fired, a dark blur shot between us. The soldier's hands drifted slowly to his side, and he collapsed flat on his back. I removed his helmet, looking the frozen and terrified man over to make sure he was still alive.

"Impeccable timing as usual, Ghost," I said.

"You should duplicate their entry key before worrying about their condition," Ghost scolded.

"Negative. They're just following orders. I'm not going to leave them to die in the desert."

Ghost flapped his wings a couple of times. One of the ways he expressed frustration.

"Your calculations are inefficient. You're trying to save thousands. Two is insignificant next to that."

I looked at him with a smile. "Then let's make it thousands plus two."

"Stubborn."

More than anyone else, he knew convincing me would require far more energy than it was worth. Instead, he approached the soldier I had knocked out with a punch, opened his beak, and sprayed more of his neurotoxin.

"Don't waste it, Ghost. We could've just tied him up or something," I said.

"This is more efficient, and I can use my small enhancer to increase production."

I sighed. This *was* more efficient. It would leave them with fewer injuries, fewer means of escape, and they'd regain control of their bodies in a day's time. Their vitals wouldn't set off any automatic alarms, and their suits would allow them to be found easily when they failed to return from their patrol. By then, I'd be deep inside the barrier.

"Fair enough," I admitted.

"Speaking of not wasting a valuable resource. You should not have used your enhancer for a trivial encounter like this. You may be vulnerable if we find ourselves fighting again soon."

"Overwhelming force was needed to avoid killing them," I clarified, as if that clarified anything.

"Again, two lives are—"

"Worth saving, Ghost. Father is going to be disappointed to learn you've taken his place. No... I'd say you're more like Mother."

Ghost tilted his head.

"I'll enlist her help to talk sense into you."

I laughed, patting the device strapped around my wrist. "I've duplicated the clearance key and added it to ours. You're welcome to try that with Mother, by the way. She's going to be disappointed to learn what I've done. She'll probably disown me."

Was that actually true?

"Why would that matter?" Ghost asked. Of course, I'd failed to consider a shadowfalcon's views on family dynamics differing from my own. They were the rarest species of animal, not only in my own adversity zone, but perhaps the whole world. It's not like anyone had studied them... aside from me. Besides, its not like they could talk or anything. Ghost being the exception, of course. That came from the experiments he had to endure at PanTech.

But the question was a fair one. Why did I care so much?

I pondered it as I dragged the two men inside the barrier, propping them up against a large rock in the shade.

"In the grand scheme of things, amidst all these calculations you're making, I guess it doesn't matter all that much," I said, not buying my own response.

"Of all the human social structures, the family is the most challenging to understand. It's no wonder PanTech sought to take it out of the equation."

"Truer words have rarely been spoken, Ghost. I've uploaded the clearance to your enhancer so you can also come and go as you please. It'll probably be best if we separate for a while. Once I put their helmets back on, these two will be fine here until the toxin wears off. Are you ready to liberate our first adversity zone?"

Ghost simply nodded before flying off again. At least I got a nod out of him this time. And I was supposedly the stubborn one?

Liberation...

A lifelong dream, which now held a meaning that hardly resembled what it once meant.

There would be no happy ending for humanity.

But freedom…

Freedom might still have a chance.

Chapter 2

Hours of walking in the desert heat brought perspective. Unwanted, but maybe not unneeded. The power suits worn by PanTech soldiers were composed of multiple bulky sections, but the bulk didn't come from poor design. The thing had its own environmental containment system. Kept you cool in the heat, and warm in the cold. It kept the body hydrated, sealed wounds, and even filtered body waste. A gross concept, but convenient for any mission. My armor, as this heat was reminding me, did very few of those things despite being more advanced. It filtered my sweat back into my body to keep me from dehydrating too quickly, but no built-in air conditioning.

It also stimulated optimal muscle use and protected me from damage. It would deflect virtually any blade and harden upon a sudden blunt impact. That wouldn't stop my organs from being turned into soup if I was hit hard enough. A rifle carried by an Adversity Management soldier would do the trick.

I pulled my black ponytail tight, wiping the sweat from my dark skin, scanning the landscape with my narrow, brown eyes.

Would Mother be proud of me for taking better care of my hair than I did when I was a teenager?

Better yet, why was this thought even crossing my mind?

"You're going in the right direction," Ghost said, swooping down and landing next to me.

"What made you think I didn't already know that?" I snapped, letting the heat get to me.

"Because you've been changing directions every few minutes. You aren't focusing."

"What?!" I shouted. "You couldn't have told me that earlier?"

"I assumed you knew what you were doing," Ghost said, flying off again.

Just a few years was all it took, though I still wasn't quite ready to admit it. It was much harder for me to keep my direction in the desert, distracted or not. Even with this suit helping a bit, I couldn't handle the heat like I once could. Barely a day into this mission and I was already doubting myself.

It probably had more to do with coming home. *This* adversity zone, in particular, was the trouble. Too many memories. Many wounds that had barely closed. In a few moments, I'd be stepping into the market where Linus, the rebel PanTech soldier I'd fallen for, was gunned down by other PanTech soldiers. I still had the nightmares sometimes.

I wondered if the village chief had stopped terrorizing the young girls here, like Linus made him promise he would. Probably not.

As the market came into sight, it became abundantly clear this village had more than just a couple of soldiers guarding it. There was one stationed at the gate, though luckily he was distracted. I'd have to take a bit of a detour.

It was coming back to me now. The layout of the village naturally popped into my mind as I approached. A less-used alleyway a bit to the side. If a soldier was stationed there, I'd have to handle the problem directly.

I sighed at the thought, veering away from the village again until I was out of sight. Once I was confident I could no longer be seen, I sat down behind a large boulder.

Ghost flew down, staring at me quietly for a moment.

"What is it, Ghost?" I asked, drawing random characters in the sand below. "If you have any questions, just ask."

"You decided it may be easier to sneak in during nightfall. There's nothing to ask," he said.

"You know, you could just ask me questions to make me feel better."

"What questions make you feel better?"

I sighed, leaning my head against the hard surface, then growled in frustration. I looked over to Ghost, thankful that he was holding together better than I was.

"I guess I just really don't know what I'm doing, or if this is even something I can do. There are a lot of adversity zones, and this is the only one I'm actually familiar with. I grew up here, but I'm struggling already."

"Human psychology is a strange concept to me. You appear to be stalling. Do you know why?"

"St-stalling?" I asked, the realization sinking in as soon as Ghost said it aloud. "Yeah… I guess I'm stalling. Sorry."

"Why are you apologizing?" Ghost asked. "This is your mission. I'm just accompanying you."

"I think I'm just apologizing to no one in particular. Myself, maybe. I guess." I picked up a small rock, drawing another animal in the sand before rubbing the image away violently with my hand and sighing. "If you want to hunt for a bit, I think I need some time to settle my mind down."

Ghost tilted his head. "Are you sure you're alright, Taylor?"

"Yeah, go ahead. I'm sure it'll be nice to hunt familiar prey again. I'm going to wait a couple of hours after dark before I sneak in. Maybe I'll take a nap until then."

Ghost hesitated a moment before flying off.

Maybe a nap is exactly what I need. I rested my head against the rock and almost instantly fell asleep.

**

I'd become a light sleeper. It seemed to be one of the side-effects of using an enhancer. Hyper-awareness of one's surroundings, often involuntarily enhanced during sleep. With the older, more powerful, brain-frying version, it wasn't unusual to hear the wings of an insect flapping across the room. The sound of a person's heartbeat before they were even close enough for a conversation. Yet, here it was a comfort, as my current observations confirmed.

I wasn't sure how long I'd been asleep. A couple of minutes, or hours. I couldn't sense Ghost, but the heartbeat of someone approaching quietly from behind. So quietly their steps were nearly silent, even as I strained my enhanced hearing to detect them.

Whether it was curiosity or animosity, I didn't know, but they were clearly trying to be very quiet and sneak up on me. Without the enhancer, I'd have no idea they were approaching.

A sudden swish in the air told me an object was being swung toward me, and I reacted accordingly. Rolling forward, I drew Twisted Key and pivoted on the balls of my feet. This person didn't wear a power suit. Pushing the enhancer again so soon could be an issue, not to mention what would happen if I started to rely on it for every little thing.

A weapon shot forward again, and I side-stepped, spinning Twisted Key in an upward arc to deflect it. Using the opening, I charged forward, but the figure dashed back with astonishing speed. An enhancer?

No, not quite. This was a regular human, but very athletic. Maybe I'd need the enhancer after all, or maybe I could hold out for Ghost. He'd be back soon. Any moment.

I was careful to attack with the side of my sword. No need to cut the person into pieces if I could help it. A moment later, I realized I was being extended the same courtesy. A counterattack struck me in the arm, the impact being largely negated by my armor, still sending me stumbling.

A follow up attack came from the spear-like weapon. Eager to stop my attacker's momentum, I caught the shaft of the spear under my arm, turning as I did and shoving my attacker off balance. However, they quickly released their own weapon and lunged forward. I had no choice but to release the spear, so it wouldn't hinder my own strike.

But the figure rushed in too quickly, landing a fierce kick to my chest. Could this be…

No, it couldn't be.

Could it?

I caught her wrist as she launched a blow toward my throat, twisting my hip and throwing her over my shoulder. To my surprise, she landed gracefully, wrapping her legs around my arm, grabbing it with her other hand, and pulling me to the ground in an arm bar. Had I not been wearing the armor I'd be in serious trouble. Sensing the hyper-extension of my elbow, the suit hardened and resisted the movement, effectively making it useless beyond restraint.

Seems I'd have to use the enhancer. Just a bit.

Shifting my weight forward, I quickly stood to my feet again, stepping my foot toward their throat. A woman.

Her reaction was quick, and she released my arm before trying a sweep. My legs didn't buckle, again thanks to the suit.

A moment later, I could hear the subtle flapping of wings closing in.

"Ghost, wait!" I shouted, causing Ghost to veer off to the side at the last moment.

"Taylor?" the woman asked with a shaky voice, pulling the scarf down from her face.

"Good to see you again, Mother," I said, smiling.

My mother stepped forward, saying nothing before pulling me into a tight embrace. I wanted to say something else, but the sound of her sobs cut me off.

"Welcome home," she finally said.

"It's good to be home," I replied, no longer able to fight back my own tears.

Chapter 3

I woke up the next morning in a bed I'd never expected to wake up in again. A basic straw mattress, which should have been nigh unusable by PanTech standards, was the most comforting thing I'd experienced in a long time. I didn't fully realize how exhausted I was until this moment. My mother had guided me down familiar alleyways, quietly smuggling me into our home where... they'd most certainly look first if they knew who they were dealing with. If they knew, but they likely didn't. Knowing who I was would've meant approaching me differently. Even if they knew all about me as a PanTech professor, they likely had no idea of my connection to this village or anyone here. Origins were rarely discussed.

A knock at my door pulled me from my thoughts.

"Breakfast will be ready soon," my mother said.

Ah, a real breakfast. Not artificial, machine-made, nutrition meals with perfect macro and micronutrient composition. I could smell it already. It made my head swim.

As I sat up in bed, I saw a fresh set of clothes lying beside me. Changing would be for the best. I could at least keep my armor on underneath. The sword, blaster, and other items could stay hidden in my room. Ghost could certainly keep himself busy until I needed him again. Considering he wasn't waiting at my bedside, something else must've gotten his attention. I wasn't worried. Ghost liked doing his own thing.

"Coming," I replied.

Could this really work?

I changed into one of my old outfits, surprised that it still fit. I'd gained a bit of muscle on my frame, but otherwise my body was almost exactly the same. After looking at myself in the mirror, I struggled momentarily with the mixed feelings toward the person looking back at me. With a quiet nod, I walked out of my room and sat at the dinner table.

Part of me hoped I'd see Ferris there, but he'd most likely been sent to some other adversity zone far, far away and fed lies about why he was there. PanTech didn't send employees back to their own zones anyway. They claimed it was to avoid favoritism toward the citizens of the zone, but it was more likely they feared a soldier not following orders to oppress someone they knew the name and face of. Easier to abuse strangers. A sad fact of human nature.

Though I knew Ferris would not be joining us, my mother still had a spot cleared for him. If he walked in, she'd only need to put a plate down and we could all be a family again like nothing ever happened. For a moment, I wondered how things would have turned out had we never agreed to join PanTech. What would life look like right now?

If only I could be so selfish. That scenario was easy to see playing out. We'd likely be in an even worse predicament than we already were. I suppose I needed to give myself some credit there.

My mother silently filled my plate, placing it in front of me with a smile.

"Your father will be a bit late, but he insisted I make you breakfast so you wouldn't need to wait for him."

"Does Father still teach?" I asked.

"Until recently. A lot has happened in the past few years, Taylor. I'll let your father tell you his part, and he'll want to hear yours. For now, focus on eating your breakfast."

I looked down. That certainly wouldn't be a problem.

Ham. Real ham left a trail of visible steam in the air, invading my nostrils with anticipated flavor. Eggs. From actual chickens. Not the nutritionally perfect, uncanny substitutes PanTech synthesized. Authentic food, with all its flaws, may as well have been a gift from the gods. I cut away a piece of the ham and slowly lifted the fork to my mouth. It was all I could do not to cry.

"A bit overwhelming, isn't it?" Mother said. "I still remember that feeling, after having spent years eating what they served at PanTech HQ. You get used to it, but then when you taste real food again..."

"I'm sorry, Mother," I said. I'm not sure why that's the thing I chose to say, of all the things going through my mind.

"You have nothing to apologize for."

"I know," I said.

I did know that, but knowing and feeling are sometimes at odds with one another.

Mother sat quietly, offering me a smile whenever I looked up from my food.

"Those were some pretty impressive moves you pulled off last night," she said. "You've become quite the athlete since you've been with PanTech. Does that mean you ended up joining Adversity Management instead of one of the science departments?"

"Something like that..." I mumbled. "I was part of Animal Research for a while, before founding my own department."

"Your own department? You became a professor then? Surely you're the youngest professor they've ever promoted." Her voice filled with involuntary pride.

"A bit younger than Elise, the College of Neuroscience professor, yes. But Mother…"

She sat across from me and took my hand in hers. "I know. You wouldn't have come into the village the way you did if all was well."

Before I could open my mouth, Father burst through the door, tossing his bag aside and rushing toward me. I stood, nearly sending my chair toppling behind me. He picked me up and spun me around. He'd aged noticeably since I'd last seen him, his beard now decorated with lines of gray.

"It's so good to see you, Taylor. How is your brother? Do you see him these days?"

I sighed, returning to my seat. "Please, get your breakfast. Both of you. I'll try to give you the abridged version."

I waited patiently while they filled their plates and sat at the table, but I could see the worry and anticipation was killing them. Father, who had always hated PanTech, was no doubt waiting to have his views validated. And for the most part, they would be.

"I've seen Ferris, but not recently. My visit here isn't authorized. The truth is there's no one left to authorize it."

"What?" Mother gasped, her face growing pale.

"I mean it has collapsed. The whole thing. PanTech HQ itself is destroyed. Only a few of us made it out alive. A lot of Adversity Management was already deployed to the zones. I'm certain that's the case for Ferris, because I didn't see him there when any of this was happening. I just don't know where he is."

I'd half expected Father to launch into an "I told you so" rant, but he seemed even more at a loss than Mother.

"Was it a rebellion?" he asked.

"PanTech's president would say so, but no. This all started with a foolish old man who dreamed of becoming immortal and was willing to destroy everything in the process. I can't claim to know every last detail but... Wait here," I said, stepping away from the table to retrieve a small pouch I'd brought with me. When I returned, I unrolled it on the table next to my plate.

"Syringes?" Mother asked, her confusion only growing.

"Part of his grand plan was a virus that could target very specific human traits. A culling of the less worthy, where almost everyone met the criteria. I can only assume he planned to shrink humanity down to a small group of immortal elites, with him at the helm."

"But things didn't work out as planned for him, did they?" Father interjected, seeming to speak mostly to himself as he struggled to process what he was being told.

"No. The virus was far deadlier to humans than anything ever created by nature or in a lab. It behaves strangely. It can seem to disappear, only to return and kill months or even a few years later. We urged them to destroy it and start over, but by then a former Adversity Management soldier, someone I... trusted, infected himself, the dogs and cats that were in my Explorers League and Adversity Management, and sent them to all the zones to act as carriers, none the wiser."

"Those strange anthropomorphic animals are the carriers?" Father asked.

"Anyone can be a carrier. The animals only carry it but aren't killed by it. They pass it to humans," I said.

"What is the mortality rate?" Mother asked. She'd been eager to ask that question, and I had wished I could avoid answering it forever.

"Guaranteed. It can't be survived."

"But you've developed a cure?" Father asked, gesturing to the line of syringes in front of him.

I paused, taking a deep breath.

"No... I've developed a vaccine that prevents the virus from becoming fatal to the host."

"I can see it on your face. What are the costs of the cure?" Mother asked.

"Complete sterilization," I said, dropping my fist on the table. "Do you understand what that means?"

They both sat quietly for a moment. Of course they understood what it meant. It didn't take a genius to reach that conclusion, but Mother and Father were both sharp.

"Is this really the end of humanity? Decline the vaccine and die, or take it and be unable to reproduce?" Father stroked his beard as he asked, as though he was hoping to reach a better conclusion. I wished that was possible. More than anything, I wanted someone more capable than me to point out something I'd been missing all along. A small flaw in my conclusion I wasn't seeing. A solution right under our noses.

But that wasn't reality. That wasn't the truth.

Father held out his arm, frowning. "Perhaps... we can develop a cure later with the time bought by your vaccine."

I took out a sterilizing wipe, along with a syringe. I wiped his arm, and quickly administered the dose.

"Considering all of those facilities are now destroyed by giant murder machines and it would take us generations to rebuild them, assuming the machines don't suddenly deploy and kill us all first..."

Mother placed a hand on my shoulder. "You did the best you could, Taylor. You're doing the best you can." She extended her own arm.

"I'm sorry…" I said, failing again to hold back my tears. "In the end, all I can do is delay the inevitable. I tried so hard. My friends too. We failed to stop any of it."

"For those who remain, this is no small thing," Father said. "There is a time for stepping back and looking at everything, and a time for stepping forward and looking closely at what is in front of you. This is that time for you. Your vaccine can ease suffering and allow children to grow up and die old as they were meant to. You said these animals aren't killed by the virus. Perhaps it is their time to inherit the world, and our opportunity to shape that world for them. We can leave them a gift, instead of a burden."

This was the most optimistic I'd ever heard my father, a true cynic, ever be in his life. I needed to hear it. More than anything, I needed to hear someone frame it exactly as he had. Maybe, in the end, I wouldn't save anyone.

But… I still had a purpose.

Chapter 4

We talked for hours about everything I experienced during my time at PanTech. All the triumphs and all the heartache. Mother regularly commented about how this or that had changed from her time there, but it seemed that few things of substance ever changed. A few small breakthroughs here and there, nearly all military-focused despite having no enemies on the entire planet I was aware of. Citizens had to be controlled, of course. Wasn't it always about control?

"You've been through so much in such a short time, Taylor," Father said, placing a hand on my shoulder.

I pointed to his beard. "Quite a bit of gray in your beard since I've been gone. I hope Mother hasn't been working you too hard."

Mother tried and failed to hold back a chuckle.

"As if anyone could force your father to do anything. If a more stubborn man exists, I've not met him."

"Oh, come now, I'm not that bad," Father said. Was he actually embarrassed? "I have been busy, yes. I've combed through the laws of this village, and I intend to oust the current chieftain. After that, the villagers will *choose* a new chief. It's been a long process, as most of our laws and customs have been obscured or are incomplete. Understandable, given PanTech just cobbled them together and made them up on a whim. It's not like they've been established naturally through many years of testing in a real, true society that emerged organically. If that were the case, then—"

"Dear..." Mother said, attempting to steer Father back on track.

"Right, I should stick to the point first. It sounds like you have a similar goal. To be honest, I just wanted to be a thorn in PanTech's side. Annoy them. Force them to step in and mend their sloppy work. Now, it seems this kind of move could be possible, if not practical. Though I can't deny a glaring reality, based on the story you just told me about the attempt to remove the president at PanTech."

I sighed. Why were any of us surprised, really?

"When it comes right down to it, if they lose, they'll use force to maintain the status quo. They'll cheat, sabotage, or outright ignore legitimate challenges or victories. Why wouldn't they do it on a smaller scale, right? Let's say you win these legal challenges, and it takes you years. How likely do you think they'll be to honor it? It sounds like you already know this, considering you just admitted you didn't think it would work when you started the whole thing."

"Go ahead and state your mind directly," he said.

"Alright. Why not just skip the line, deal with the occupation, and watch the chief grovel for his life when he knows no one is left to protect him?"

Father stroked his beard, letting the suggestion sink in.

"What about supplies? Can this village really survive independently without trade?" Mother asked.

"I could establish that trade myself, if it's needed," I said.

"If it's needed," Father echoed. "I don't believe it would be, and I'm not sure establishing relationships with other zones so quickly is the right move. You've mentioned they have very different levels of technology. A zone with much higher levels of technology could wipe us out in a day if they wanted to."

"Even though that's true, why would they want to?" Mother asked, shrugging as she did. Mother was a cynical person by the standards of most, but compared to Father...

"Why did the president of PanTech, arguably one of the most brilliant men to ever live, undo all his life's work and achievements on some deluded mission to become immortal?

Humans are not always logical. Perhaps they'd seek to become the new PanTech, trying to fill that power vacuum. Perhaps they'd fear others one day becoming a threat. Fools are aplenty. I'd dare not underestimate a man's capacity to be foolish."

"Or a woman's," I added. "You can keep playing chess in your mind, but I'll be forced to play a different game. My lab, which I need to keep making these vaccines, must stay hidden and shouldn't be in one place for too long. The virus limits the amount of time I can stay in a single zone. Unfortunately, I'll have to move on as soon as they're dealt with here. And I'll have to do it quickly."

Father closed his eyes and stroked his beard. This wasn't what he was hoping to hear.

"Understood. You don't have time to participate in the long game here. You're right."

"Remove PanTech control and make my case for vaccinating the population. Do you think the chieftain will even try to remain in power after Adversity Management is kicked out?"

Father shrugged. "Your guess is as good as mine on what that fool will do."

"Have you thought about going and speaking with him?" Mother asked.

"Diplomacy is the first thing on my mind… sometimes, but I think it's too likely he'll just turn me in to Adversity Management right away. I need some time to walk around the village and get a feel for the situation with Pan-Tech's end of things. Some of the animals were part of my division and will most likely help me. There might be a few Adversity Management soldiers who are willing to see reason as well."

"What about all the people who will recognize you?" Father asked. A fair question.

"I don't think most here are going to think twice. My eyes are the only thing that set me apart from a completely average person here, and I was pretty introverted before. The few people who recognize me, I'll just tell them I'm visiting or something. They won't care enough to dig deeper. Cara, I plan to tell everything."

"Are you sure that's a good idea?" Father asked, shifting uncomfortably.

I wasn't sure, and I was frustrated with myself for it.

"If there's a lesson I've learned the hard way in my time at PanTech, it's that you should always lean on friends when you can. The positives will usually outweigh the negatives. If someone betrays your trust, others can help you through it. I won't make the same mistakes again. If Cara wants to help, I'll welcome it."

Mother placed a hand on my shoulder, smiling.

"You've grown up so much, Taylor. I'm glad all that's happened hasn't poisoned your view of the world."

I wasn't so much concerned about the world. My view of the world had been poisoned. So much of it was rotten. There would always be people like the president. My father was absolutely correct, and I knew these things would emerge from liberating the zones. But what choice did we have? I had to focus on doing the most good I could, not delude myself into thinking I could fix everything. That, after this, everyone would get along and live peacefully together.

"If everyone can understand we're one generation from extinction, maybe they'll give peace a chance," I said, despite not believing it myself.

"I suspect many of them won't believe it at first, but they will in time. Our abilities to convince ourselves of a different reality can only carry us so far," Father said.

"It still hasn't sunk in for me. I'm not sure it ever will. I've had plenty of time to think about it, and it still feels like a dream. Like every time I wake up, I'll realize it was all my imagination. The others who escaped, my friends, I think they're all feeling the same way. Just taking it one day at a time. But we'll be okay... won't we?"

The last line was meant to be a declaration, but turned into a question as it left my lips.

I'd desperately wanted to believe it was true.

"We'll be okay," Father said, putting an arm around my shoulder and hugging me close.

"Go see Cara. It'll do you good," Mother said, placing an arm around my father and pulling us all close together. Something so uncharacteristic of Mother. Seems she'd changed more than any of us. "They've made things harder for Cara since you left, but I will not tell her story in her place."

Strength Through Adversity had long since lost its appeal.

Or… maybe it was more true than ever.

Chapter 5

If anyone could help me, I knew it would be Cara. She'd stuck by me through everything. She'd helped me run the clinic when the old veterinarian passed away. She comforted me when Linus was killed. She helped me save Ghost when he was injured. When I joined a rebel group in the village, she supported me then too. Even helped me join. Then, when I learned they were the ones who set Linus up, she apologized. I'd always trusted Cara and never for a moment suspected she had anything to do with it. I'd made great friends since leaving for Pan-Tech, but always missed Cara.

Entering the market, I scanned it from end to end, instantly relieved there were no soldiers in sight. I walked as casually as I could, hoping no one would stop and recognize me as I made my way to the veterinarian stall.

"Hello," I said as I approached. A crouching figure had been struggling with a sack of feed on the ground. I'd assumed it was Cara. Instead, it was a young man, likely around fourteen or fifteen years old.

"Hello," he offered. "What can I help you with today?"

"I was hoping to talk to Cara," I said, looking all around the stall as I did.

"She's not here. She's not feeling well, so she stayed home today."

"That's not like Cara. She never misses work," I said, prompting a furrowed brow from the young man.

"Huh? She misses a lot, and barely does anything when she's here. She mostly just tells me what to do." Noticing my irritation, he amended his statement. "Which... I don't blame her for! Those PanTech—" He stopped, composing himself. I knew *that* look all too well. Poor guy was about to explode. "Cara's experiencing additional adversity to strengthen her character." He smiled, but his eyes gave away his true feelings.

"Has she moved to a different house in the past few years?" I asked. I'd learned to mask my own feelings well. Besides, I'd be dealing with them soon enough.

"Depends on who's asking," he grunted, folding his arms.

I liked this kid's spirit.

"It's okay. I'm an old friend. You could say... I've also been dealing with PanTech for the past few years. This is the first opportunity I've had to reach out to her in a while."

He eyed me up and down for a moment before relaxing. A bit.

"No, she's in the same house. Don't cause her more problems, you hear?"

"I won't," I said, hoping that would be the truth. I was a magnet to trouble already and now I was looking for it.

As I walked away from the stall and toward Cara's home a short distance away, I considered turning around and deciding on a different course of action. Involving Cara felt wrong, but I had to know. I needed to talk to her and see how she was doing. The anxiety built inside of me and seemed to grow with each step. I barely noticed the two soldiers walking right by me in their power suits. I only saw them as they passed, out of the corner of my eye. I turned, even though it would've been better not to. Nothing identifiable. Just two regular soldiers, and they didn't notice me any more than I'd noticed them.

I knocked on Cara's door, but there was no answer. As one of the soldiers stopped and began to turn, I decided to enter instead of risking being recognized.

The room was dark, with curtains pulled. A small figure sat in a chair. No, this couldn't be Cara!

I rushed to the window, pulling back curtains to allow the morning light to flood in. The skeletal figure awoke, held up a hand to shield her eyes and recoiled from the light.

"Cara?" I asked, rushing to her side and grabbing her hand.

"T… Taylor?" she replied. I knew it was her voice.

I gripped her hand tightly, almost too tightly. I could only stomach a glance before competing emotions flooded my chest.

She'd been starved to the brink of death. Her arms barely had enough muscle mass left to lift them. How she walked at all was amazing to me. Her hair was thin. Her eyes were dark, and her heavy lids fluttered slowly.

My eyes grew hazy, and a flood of tears poured down my cheeks.

"Yeah, it's me, Taylor," I said, choking on the words as I said them.

She reached out slowly and put her arm around me, her eyes welling with tears of her own.

"I thought I'd never see you again," she said in a weak voice.

For every tear that fell from my eye, it may as well have been fuel dripping into a flame. There were times when I hated PanTech more than ever—this was one of those times.

I stood to my feet, releasing her hand and clenching my fists at my side.

"Don't rush off. Won't you sit with me for a while?" Cara asked, sensing my intentions as always. As though we hadn't lost a single day. I sighed and sat on the floor next to her.

"Of course," I said, wiping my eyes with my sleeve. "I'm sorry."

"None of this is your fault, Taylor."

"It's because of the rebel group, isn't it? They implicated you in it."

"Still not your fault," she insisted. Even as her words tried to deescalate my anger, hearing her weak voice only served to build it higher. Cara was one of the sweetest girls to ever live. She should've been able to take over the vet clinic properly. She should've been able to continue practicing her leatherworking, and improving the lives of the people here. Instead...

"Fine, but I'm still going to fix it," I growled.

"Why are you here?" she asked.

That's right. I'd completely forgotten why I'd visited in the first place, but that didn't matter.

Was she well enough to give the vaccine? Because of her current condition, the virus would kill her quickly. Likely before any warning signs could be noticed. But if I caused her to go through all this, only to show up and kill her with my own two hands... I could never forgive myself.

"Taylor, are you alright?" she asked.

"Don't ask me if I'm alright. Not after everything you've been through, Cara." I reached into my pocket, pulling out one of the small devices I'd smuggled in. "This'll hurt a bit," I said, holding her finger and giving it a small poke. A tiny bead of blood pooled on her fingertip.

"What's that thing?" she asked.

"A little something I took as a souvenir from PanTech. It analyzes the blood. Are they starving you, or is it something in your food?"

"They're putting something in my food... I think. I don't know. I don't get much food either."

I eyed the readings. They'd been adding a drug to her food to block nutritional absorption beyond a certain amount. It's how they'd kept her in this weak, but stable condition. I entered a bit of data, rewrote the formula, and...

"Let me see your finger one more time," I insisted.

She complied, and I stuck her again.

"Ouch. Twice? I expected PanTech to be more advanced."

"This drug is of PanTech origin. Think of it as a tiny machine. For these types of drugs, PanTech employees with access to the right tools can easily rewrite them to perform a different task. Nothing's going to solve this overnight. Unfortunately, I'll have to return mass to your body slowly so it doesn't cause your system shock. You'll start feeling more energetic right away, but you'll need to hide that."

"I wish you hadn't done that, Taylor. You're amazing, but I wish you hadn't."

I frowned, gently embracing her.

"I know you're scared. I'm going to take care of this village's PanTech problem, and then I'm moving on to another. The whole organization has collapsed, and…" I unrolled my syringes. "I'm sorry, I'm going to have to give this one to you in your neck."

She hesitated at first, leaning away from me. "No…"

"Please trust me, Cara. The virus they let loose… if you contract it in your state, it'll kill you before I have time to vaccinate you. Before you even show symptoms."

"A virus? what? No. Give me some time to think. If they find out you helped me they'll make things so much worse for me. Please, just go."

"I'll go but… just this one last thing."

The nanomachines in her system were a blessing in disguise. Now that I'd rewritten them to stabilize her body, it could work in tandem with the vaccine and prevent it from putting too much strain on her body. It was safe, and I couldn't miss my chance.

"I won't force you, Cara… but please," I pleaded.

Cara took a deep breath, placing a hand over her eyes. She nodded.

I placed the needle in her neck, ejecting the fluid slowly. She jumped a bit, making a pitiful, painful whimper as the needle entered.

I would make sure someone paid dearly for this. Very dearly.

"Who decided this punishment for you?" I asked.

"The mayor and the current commander I think," she said as I removed the needle. "Don't… Taylor."

I put my hand on her cheek, wiping away one of her tears with my thumb.

"I'll be back to visit you soon, okay?"

Cara simply nodded, and although her words were kind, she was clearly terrified I was going to create more trouble for her.

I was going to create a whole lot of trouble. That much was very true.

But it wasn't going to be for her.

Chapter 6

Things often got worse before they got better. At least, that's the lie we told ourselves to justify things getting worse. I wasn't sure I'd ever made things better for Cara, the way she had for me, but there was no way I was about to let PanTech treat her that way now that I was here. It didn't matter if I had to throw plans out the window and start slicing my way through the problem. I was on borrowed time anyway. Being smart was all well and good, but it was a luxury. A luxury I kept debating whether I even had.

As soon as I stepped out of Cara's house, I heard a commotion. Shouting near the market where I'd just been, and several people hastily moving in the opposite direction. That was telling. If it was just a fight, there'd be a crowd. The fact people were running meant it wasn't worth the danger of sticking around and watching.

I moved against the flow of people, finding myself a vantage point where I could observe without being observed. The young man from before was still in the veterinary stall, so I joined him, acting as though I belonged there.

"Cara's feeling a bit better today. I used to run this clinic, by the way. Mind if I join you?"

I said, saying the words but not really giving him the opportunity to answer.

"You're Taylor? But... how? And I wouldn't be sticking around here if I were you. It could get ugly. Some of the soldiers are bickering again."

"I'm visiting," I said casually. It wasn't a lie, after all. "And what do you mean when you say ugly? Have they fought before? That's unusual."

"*Was* unusual," he corrected. "Not as much anymore. Last week one of them actually killed another. Can you believe that also happened here a few years ago?"

I guess he didn't know all that much about me.

"Yeah... I was here for it," I said, struggling to speak the words despite the time that had passed. The image flooded back into my mind every time it was mentioned. Linus, protecting me, shot and killed by two other Adversity Management soldiers. It didn't matter to me that he took both of them with him. The nightmares had lessened a bit, but never went away.

"Oh... sorry," he said, immediately regretting that reference.

"Don't worry. Tell me about what's going on right now," I said, wanting to remove that subject from my thoughts as quickly as possible.

"Well, I can't exactly say. They don't really air their dirty laundry for the villagers to see. The best I can tell, it's a problem with these strange animal people. They don't seem to get along with each other. The cats don't get along with the dogs, and there are two different uniforms. The different uniforms don't seem to get along with the others either."

Explorers League! My faction. Finally, I had something small to be hopeful about. If some of the dogs and cats from my Explorers League were here... I'd still need to find some way to communicate with them without the others knowing. That would probably be nearly impossible. I'd have to wait for my chance, or just hope they were willing to follow me when the time came. Farle might've been a backstabbing jerk, but he may have unwittingly spread allies throughout all the zones for me.

The two soldiers in the market were both wearing white power suits, which meant Adversity Management. That armor would also be a problem. The Explorers League was formed around exploring abandoned areas and destroying machines. Not people, and certainly not Adversity Management. It was a game of Rock, Paper, Scissors we were bound to lose if we approached it directly.

"We need to make contact with the others," one cat shouted to the dog standing near him.

"You *need* to shut your mouth and follow orders," the dog replied. "We'll make contact when we're told to make contact."

"Who exactly is going to tell you, idiot?" the cat hissed.

"Not you, hairball," the dog barked.

"Okay, that's enough," a clearly distressed human who had the misfortune of standing between them said. Even obscured by bulky armor, his anxiety was clear. His posture was pleading, and he seemed almost desperate to avoid a confrontation.

"No one asked you," the dog shouted.

"If you don't have an opinion of your own, maybe you should go babysit somewhere else," the cat added.

Ah, something they can agree on. They don't like humans. Being human, that fact wouldn't exactly be to my benefit. However, it meant they were likely disorganized and weren't cohesive. I remembered how my own cats and dogs were like that in the beginning. However, we eventually overcame it. Cats and dogs from Explorers League got along great… or at least I hoped they still did. Why hadn't I spotted any of them so far?

"How often do you see the ones with different uniforms?" I asked the young man.

"Not often. Not in a while, actually. I think they're off doing their own thing somewhere nearby. Inside the barrier, I assume, but I don't really know."

Could that mean there was machine activity nearby, or did they just not want to be around Adversity Management? Or, maybe they were driven out by force. I hoped that wasn't the case. That would mean I missed my chance. As long as they were okay...

"Just seems like they're squabbling. Why did everyone run?" I asked.

Before he had a chance to answer, the answer came to me. The cat in the group walked over, staring me up and down.

"Got something to say, human?"

I held up my hands in surrender. "No, sir. I'm sorry."

He narrowed his eyes. "Hey, do I know you?"

Not good.

"I think we've met a couple of times here in the market," I lied.

"That's probably it. You're on thin ice. I don't like being gossiped about by grass eaters, and that goes for humans or dogs."

"Yeah, you're so tough. Our job is to manage this place, not brag to the merchants in their stalls," the dog teased.

"I'm *not* bragging," the cat growled.

"Okay! Okay... let's move on with our patrol," the human pleaded. His tone was so full of defeat I almost pitied him. No, I did pity him. A little.

"I've got my eyes on you," the cat said to me as he turned and stormed off with the others.

The young man took a deep breath and exhaled. "That was close."

"Adversity Management has always had its fault, but insubordination is extremely rare and usually dealt with swiftly. Is there no commander here?"

"Oh, the commander is the worst of them all. He rarely even wears his power suit. Spends all his time with young women from the village and doesn't seem to care about his duties. And they thought the redhead from a few years ago was bad…"

The redhead from a few years ago. He must mean Frelya. She'd come such a long way as a person. I remembered how much I hated her when I was just a villager, when Linus was killed and she didn't seem to care. She was violent, and snapped at every little thing. Far worse than that cat. And yet, somehow she became one of my best friends and… I found myself missing her, and hoping she was okay. Hoping she'd survived.

"Frelya was certainly a handful," I said. "Tell me more about this current commander."

"There's nothing more to tell," the young man said with a shrug. "He lets these squabbles happen all the time, and as long as no one dis-respects him to his face he couldn't care less. Isn't that normal with PanTech?"

Yeah, I guess it was…

"What's your name?" I asked.

"Barth," he said.

I laughed. I couldn't help it.

"Hey, what's so funny?" he asked, frown-ing.

"I knew someone named Barth. I'm not sure I'd want to be named after him, but it's a good name. He was quite the accomplished fellow."

"Gee, thanks. Also, you don't actually work here, so do you mind getting out of the stall so I can at least?"

"Say, why don't you hire me?" I asked.

It seemed a lot could be observed in the mar-ket, and it gave me a chance to blend into plain sight. After all, I knew what I was doing as a veterinarian and wouldn't look out of place. Villagers would ask questions, but they wouldn't want to talk around the soldiers. Maybe I should watch what I say around pretty young women, by the sound of it. Probably no need to worry about anyone else.

"Hire you?" he asked, chuckling. "Hire you…" He paused, starting to give it serious thought. "Well I can't really pay you."

"I owe Cara," I said. I did.

"Well… if you want to volunteer here I guess I can't stop you. You seem to know what you're doing, that's for sure. Maybe stay quiet the next time the PanTech people walk by though?"

"No promises," I said.

He sighed.

"Fine… you can start by unloading that feed," he said, motioning to the cart behind me.

"You got it, boss."

Now we were getting somewhere.

Chapter 7

The next day, I showed up bright and early to the vet clinic. Barth was already tending to an injured goat, wrapping its leg.

"That's a bit too tight," I said quietly, so the customer wouldn't hear.

"Thanks," he replied.

The older man stood above us, bouncing his leg impatiently.

"This gonna take long?"

"As long as it takes," I said sharply.

He wiped his nose, eyeing me for a moment.

"Say, aren't you the one who ran this clinic a few years ago? I thought you went off to be a big shot at PanTech."

I grinned. "I accomplished everything there was to accomplish. Got bored and decided to come back home."

"Wow, that's impressive," he replied, his tone dripping with sarcasm.

Thankfully, he didn't press beyond that, and I knew a cranky old guy like that wasn't going to be making small talk with the soldiers.

Barth handed the lead back to the man and nodded. He dropped several coins in Barth's hand and quickly walked away. Not a word of thanks.

Even though I had only been here a few days, I couldn't help but feel like I was wasting more time than I had. Despite carefully studying every random villager I came into contact with, this virus would not be easy to spot. It mimicked natural illnesses. It might look like a common cold in one person, a heart attack, kidney failure, or simply going to bed one day and never waking up. The only symptoms I could recognize early were... any symptoms. This would lead to so many false positives, but none of that mattered if I could get the vaccine distributed. Then there was the issue of supply. This was a small village, but in a bigger city...

"You know that guy?" Barth asked.

"Huh? Oh, yeah. I know a lot of people here a little. I just wasn't especially close to anyone outside my family. And Cara."

"Cara talked about you a lot."

I frowned. "Yeah? Knowing her she probably said all sorts of nice things I didn't deserve."

Barth nodded. "Yep!"

"You didn't have to agree so enthusiastically," I said.

"You said it, not me." Out of the corner of his eye, he spotted something that wiped his smile away. "Oh, come on..."

It was a soldier. A human one, walking straight at us.

"If something happens, don't try to help. Just run," I said.

"Wait… do you know something I don't?"

"Lots of things," I replied, sounding as snarky as I could.

"H-how can I help you?" Barth asked.

He removed his helmet, setting it aside, revealing shoulder-length dark brown hair and light brown eyes. Slightly tanned skin. I didn't recognize him, but he seemed to recognize me. If he'd intended to be hostile, the last thing he would've done was remove his helmet. I relaxed a bit, placing a hand on Barth's shoulder.

"Any word from HQ, Professor?" he asked.

"It's mostly smoke and rubble," I replied. "What were your last orders?"

"Secure the zones and stand by. Do not interfere with the virus. Do not interfere with deployed machines. Arrest or kill insurrectionists if they appear."

"I see…" I said, suddenly finding myself on edge again. "Mind keeping my presence under wraps? You know as well as I do that I'm on that list."

"You should've thought about that before you knocked out two of our soldiers at the barrier. I just want answers," he said. He looked lost and defeated. The last thing he was looking for was a fight with me. This sounded like the same man from yesterday, so maybe he'd gotten his fill of fighting.

"What do you want to know?" I asked.

"Is anyone still alive? Why have we been told not to return?"

"One question at a time. And let's keep this conversation brief since someone could walk up on us at any moment."

"We have five minutes until the window opens for the next patrol through this market," he said.

I nodded. Good, he'd at least planned this.

"There are survivors, but the virus is the biggest danger right now. That battle is already lost. They don't want you to return because they are afraid you'll join the resistance there. Most of Adversity Management still at HQ defected immediately and fought against the machines, covering the escape of the survivors. At this point, even if you did return, there likely isn't much to return to. You could join the survivors camped outside the walls and protect them from what's to come, but I think anyone who hasn't gotten out already is…" I froze on the last word. "Even if they *are* still alive, there's no getting in to save them."

"You don't know that!" he snapped. The sudden intensity of his statement caught me off guard, but it was easy to read between the lines.

He was taking a risk just talking to me and was disobeying multiple orders at once.

"Got someone back at HQ you care about, huh? Well... me too, and I'm sorry. The one who released the president's virus did a great job, but luckily made a few mistakes along the way. The first was destroying the communication. He meant to make it impossible to warn against the spread of the virus, but it also made it impossible for the president to organize Adversity Management. My Explorers League is spread out all over the place. I need to find—"

"What are you doing, Conway?" a familiar cat's voice called out. I looked up, realizing we were being flanked by that same dog and cat. For hating each other, they sure seemed to stick together.

"Apologizing to this lady for your rudeness yesterday," he replied.

"With your helmet off?" he asked.

"Humans prefer eye contact," Conway said.

"Is this human girl cute or ugly?" the cat muttered.

Conway looked at me, panicked, probably hoping for some kind of hint as to how I wanted him to answer.

"Most beautiful girl in the village," I said. "How have you managed to overlook me so far?"

"She's so ugly it makes me sick. Seriously. The goat I just bandaged up was prettier than her," Barth said.

The cat and dog burst out laughing. Then laughed more. And more. Finally, I joined in, as did Conway. Guess Barth was convincing. I gave Conway a wink, hoping he understood.

"Leave this poor ugly creature alone so she can return to her work," the cat finally said. Ouch.

"Alright," Conway said.

He put his helmet back on, and the three walked away.

"What were you thinking?" Barth scolded. "Are you insane?"

"Aww, you really think I'm ugly?"

"No!" He scratched his head, looking away for a moment.

I laughed. Shouldn't have teased him like that.

"It will save me time to meet with the commander. That's all. And it doesn't seem like he's interested in talking to anyone who isn't a pretty girl."

Barth sighed. "I don't like it... my friend's sister has been there for two weeks now. There are girls who have been there for months. Trust me, that's the last place you want to go."

"You were listening to me when I told Conway about what happened at PanTech HQ, right?"

"I just don't want you to end up like my friend's sister, or Cara. You're just a regular person. They've got power armor, numbers, weapons. Everyone does what they say because they're too afraid not to. There's no point in throwing your life away."

I placed my hands on his shoulders and smiled.

"Barth... don't underestimate what a regular person is capable of. The clock is ticking. The virus is already here, dormant. Every day I waste is a day I won't have later, to save another zone. If their commander is behaving this way, he doesn't seem to care all that much one way or another. If I can reason with him, it's possible we can come to an understanding. Maybe he's not as bad as everyone thinks he is."

"Somehow I doubt that's the case..." he said.

I felt the same way. A PanTech commander going on an ego trip wasn't unheard of at all. The enhancers they use claw at the edges of the mind. It can change personalities or exacerbate psychological problems. Even though they chose commanders with high mental fortitude, it seemed to make little difference. Humans are humans, and we all have problems.

"Thank you for sticking up for me, regard-less. You're a good guy, Barth," I said, patting him on top of his head.

"Hey, I'm not ten," he said, swatting my hand away. "But you're welcome. And… if you really want to move things along quickly you could try talking to the chief. He recruits most of the girls for the commander."

"Oh, I'm sure he does," I said, sighing.

The problem was… I wasn't sure I could even stomach a single look at that man without snapping his neck.

Maybe calling it a problem was the wrong way to look at it.

Felt more like a solution to me.

Chapter 8

Although I questioned my own restraint, seeking out the village chief *was* the best solution. Even if Conway understood my signal, there was no telling how much influence he had with the commander. After all, a soldier who puts his own interests ahead of the organization's likely wasn't their first choice for confidence. That he was a potential ally was good enough. He was in a hurry to leave the village and save… whoever it was he'd deluded himself into believing he could save.

Surprised by my own thoughts, I paused as my foot touched the sand. I really was one to talk. As someone trying to complete another, even more impossible task, I was in no position to pass judgment on someone else. Besides, what if Frelya really was still alive? What if she really could be saved?

No. Frelya, of all people, would not want me dwelling on it. Not when my mission was right in front of me and required every ounce of my focus.

I knocked on the chieftain's door and braced myself.

A young, dark-haired girl answered.

"Sorry, the chieftain's not accepting any new girls at the moment," she said, sneering.

As she started to close the door, I caught it.

"I'm here on business," I said.

She glanced at the door, surprised by my strength. She tried again to force it closed, but I didn't let it budge. No enhancer needed.

"I'll decide who is to be turned away-uh," the familiar voice of the chieftain came from another room, creeping closer.

At last, he appeared. The slight waddle in his step he had before was now more pronounced. Unsurprising, given he'd gained a bit more weight since last I saw him. Still one of the only overweight men in a village with barely enough to eat. Same fake accent too. Of all the insufferable people I'd met since leaving the village, arrogant, self-absorbed jerks throughout the upper ranks of PanTech, I could not recall a single one I disliked more than the chieftain. Even PanTech's president, truly an evil man, could at least be admired for his ruthless competence.

"Remember me?" I asked, stepping inside and closing the door behind me. With the look on his face, an answer wasn't necessary.

This was very much against the rules, but a man like the chieftain only spoke one kind of language. I needed to show him I felt I was above the rules, or he wouldn't be remotely interested in what I had to say.

"I uh… yes I seem to recall—" He'd begun sweating before he could even complete the sentence. Or maybe he'd already been sweating.

I stepped forward, grabbing him by the collar of his shirt, pulling him close to my face, our noses nearly touching.

"You didn't keep your promise to Linus," I said.

The two girls in the room with us scampered off to another part of the home. Although not exactly a mansion, the chieftain's home could've been considered one when compared to the flimsy structures other villagers were forced to live in.

"No, uh, I have. These girls are here voluntarily-uh," he said, forcing a grin.

Ignoring his statement, I pressed my point.

"But I might be willing to overlook that. A favor for a favor, you could call it."

I released him, sending him stumbling, nearly falling before regaining his balance.

"You're the same foolish girl you always were, I see. Big talk and nothing to back it up."

"How do you suppose I'm here?" I asked. "You know it's forbidden for employees to return to their own adversity zone. Yet, here I am. Don't you wonder how that's possible?"

He swallowed hard. "I uh… well perhaps you are breaking the rules, or they've simply changed it-uh."

"PanTech professors follow a different set of rules. We answer only to the president. Not to the underlings you're accustomed to dealing with, and certainly not to insects like yourself."

"What do you want?" he asked after a brief silence. Seems I was speaking his language well enough.

"First, tell me what you know about the current commander. I'm here to investigate him, which is why I'm dressed the way I am. Your cooperation will be rewarded, and your discretion is appreciated."

"One would think you'd already know everything there is to know—" he began.

"When I'm interested in answering your questions, I'll tell you. Now answer mine," I said, cutting him off.

"Right-uh. He's a fairly agreeable sort. Though, in other ways he is much like Frelya was. Not so much interested in his official duties. He would prefer others handle things for him. He likes the girls of this village. As long as I send them to him, he leaves the duties of running this village to me."

"Do you know what happens to the girls after they're sent to him?" I asked. I almost regretted asking.

"I do not know-uh. He has never told me. He sends soldiers to escort them to his encampment and they do not return."

"How do I become one of those girls?" I asked.

"You uh… want to become one of the girls?"

"I didn't ask you to repeat what I just said," I growled.

"I select. That's all. He does not seem to be picky. Soldiers report he has been satisfied with every one I have offered. I have never spoken to him personally-uh."

"When is the next visit?" I asked.

"Today," he said, with a tone suggesting I should have known that.

"Good. What do I need to do?"

He scoffed. "There isn't enough time to prepare you today. Perhaps with next week's girls."

"There you go, offering your input again," I scolded.

"Fine! Priscilla, come here!" he shouted, clapping his hands.

The girl who answered the door reappeared, giving me another, even meaner glare.

"Yeah?"

The chieftain gestured to me. "Please escort Taylor to the back with the other girls. Do what you can to make her presentable. She'll be leaving with today's shipment."

"I'll do what I can, but I'm not a miracle worker," Priscilla said, rolling her eyes. "I remember her now. The one with the weird eyes."

"The commander is not from our zone. No doubt he will appreciate a more… exotic appearance," the chieftain said, looking at me with a smile, as though I should be thankful for his validation.

"Please, do the best you can with my weird eyes. We're on a schedule here," I said.

Priscilla rolled her eyes again, motioning for me to follow her.

We entered a large room in the back of the home. A large bathroom with a large shower, much too big to be in the home of a single person. I recognized many aspects of the room as being far too advanced for what should be in this adversity zone. If I had to guess, powered by solar with a large battery to back it up.

Several nude and semi-nude women were lined up, either being scrubbed, dressed in the village's more formal clothing, or something else.

"Undress," Priscilla ordered. "You smell like animals."

I considered playing along, but decided against it. I had several gadgets hidden carefully in my clothing, not least of all the device I

LIBERATION SAGA: VOLUME 1 | 79

needed to accurately diagnose the virus. Far too valuable to lose. I'd take my chances. If his soldiers decided I smelled too much like... animals for their commander, I'd convince them with force.

"The chieftain already said the man isn't picky. Just tell me where to wait."

Priscilla sighed. "Fine. At least let me do your hair and makeup."

I relented, sitting in a chair facing the bathroom's large mirror.

"Something to accentuate my *exotic* eyes, please," I said, doing the best I could to sound remotely serious.

"Whatever you say," she replied, quickly going to work. She certainly wasn't Mother, but I had to admit her makeup skills weren't half bad.

"What's your story?" I asked.

"What do you care?" she answered.

"I wouldn't have asked if I wasn't interested. I don't care for small talk."

She paused a moment, seeming to consider and reconsider her snappy retort she was no doubt cooking up.

"Nothing much. I failed the exam. My parents died. My little brother's been sick since he was little and needs special medicine. But hey, at least I'm beautiful."

She sped through the story like she was making a sales pitch without a product.

"Let me guess. The chieftain can get this special medicine for you. And in exchange…"

"Do I really need to spell it out for you?" she said, her glare returning.

"I hope your brother appreciates what you do for him," I said.

"He doesn't," Priscilla snapped, her mood further darkening. "Everyone looks down on me for being here. Him included. He's smart, though. When he passes the exam and goes to PanTech, he'll be able to get the medicine he needs there. I won't need to get it for him anymore. Spoiled brat can get it himself."

I tensed. I wanted to tell her that no medicine would be needed. That PanTech was perfectly capable of curing any common illness or genetic disease with a snap of their finger. That they simply let people endure them for what more or less amounts to sport. Adversity. Suffering builds character. That's how they justified it.

That was last month, however. Now, there was no PanTech waiting for anyone with hopes like her or her brother. No cures. No more exams would be held. I didn't have the heart to tell her. I could see this thought, this hope, was all that was keeping her going right now. She needed to hold on to it, if just a bit longer.

"That's admirable," I said. "You're a good person."

She sighed, leaning in front of me and examining my makeup.

"And your eyes are prettier than I thought, I guess. I guess you'll pass. Barely. Anyway, go and tell the chieftain you're ready and that we decided the animal stink added charm."

I laughed, even though she didn't intend it to be funny.

Time to put the charms Mother taught me to use.

I'd have this commander eating from the palm of my hand.

Chapter 9

Two other girls sat on a bench outside with me. One seemed excited, while the other bounced her knee nervously.

"You're awfully calm," the red-haired girl with the bouncing knee said.

I looked up, not sure if she was talking to me or the brown-haired girl beside her.

I pointed to myself. "Me?"

"Yep. How are you able to stay so calm?"

I thought about it for a moment but couldn't think of an eloquent answer that wasn't an outright lie. "I'm nervous too," I said. Even if it was for different reasons, this was true. "What do you know about where we're going?"

"Not many girls actually get sent off to the commander. I've heard the chieftain exaggerates and tells stories, hoping more approach him. Best I can tell, it's only been a few dozen since he came here."

"A few dozen is a lot," the brunette beside her said.

I nodded. It certainly was a lot, but based on the rumors I was expecting more than a hundred.

"And no one's ever returned?" I asked.

"Not that I'm aware of," the redhead replied, followed by a nod from the brunette.

A soldier approached, removing his helmet. It was Conway.

"I had a feeling I'd see you today," he said.

"What can I say? I don't like wasting time I don't have. Good to see you again, Conway."

"You two know each other?" the redhead asked.

"We met at the market yesterday. I was helping out at the vet clinic."

"Wait a minute," the brunette said, standing up. "You're Taylor. I thought I recognized you. I thought you passed the exam and went to Pan-Tech."

I shrugged, standing and nodding to Conway. "I'm on vacation."

"Vacation?" the redhead asked, tilting her head. "No one else has ever come back for a vacation."

"Maybe it's the same as how no one's ever come back from joining the commander. They're having so much fun they forget where they came from."

Conway laughed.

Was it really that funny?

"Okay, girls, let's get moving," he said, motioning for us to follow him, locking his helmet back on.

Guess that meant I wouldn't be able to ask questions along the way. Not that I could anyway with these other girls with us.

"What's the commander like?" the redhead asked.

"Remulo? He's... hard to describe. It's better for you to decide for yourself after you meet him."

***

Shortly after leaving the outskirts of the village, we boarded a vehicle. Another strange, unexpected turn of events. Adversity Management was highly discouraged from introducing technology to citizens beyond what they were familiar with in their zones. Was this because they knew no one would return from this trip? Either that, or a complete disregard for rules and regulations. Either option fit the rumors. This commander, Remulo, seemed to care very little about the rules.

I did the best I could to memorize the route. Although this zone wasn't massive, being able to follow a direct route to and from the Adversity Management camp would save me time. Regardless of what was going on with the other girls, I wasn't planning for an extended stay. I wasn't going to ignore what was going on there either. Too many eggs in one basket.

"We're here," Conway said, stepping out of the vehicle and opening the door for us.

I made sure to go last, taking my time and absorbing my surroundings. At first glance, nothing was amiss. It wasn't unlike Frelya's camp I visited several years ago. Supplies piled up. Tents spread around. Some soldiers were having a meal, playing cards, or chatting. Though, it wasn't long before things became a bit stranger.

"Hello, and welcome!" a young woman with freckles said. She was dressed in a PanTech uniform but something was odd about it. Normally they had ranks or insignias, but her uniform seemed almost decorative in a way. Like a costume. "My name's Haley, and I'll be your guide today!"

She reminded me of someone, but I couldn't quite put my finger on it. Maybe I recognized her from the village.

Conway removed his helmet and raised an eyebrow, which could have been a warning for me to brace myself. That's how I interpreted it at least.

Haley continued. "I understand it's your first day and you're probably really nervous. I bet you've heard all kinds of awful rumors about what life is like here, but I promise that if you keep an open mind you'll be pleasantly surprised."

She turned, motioning for us to follow her. Ah, now I remembered what felt so familiar about this. She reminded me of the onboarding specialists at PanTech. Those given the task of acclimating newcomers to the culture shock, were always overly positive and chipper like this girl. They gave me the creeps.

She led us into a large tent, and the smell of baked goods immediately assaulted my senses. Not that it was unwelcome.

"Here's the bakery! You'll get to sample all sorts of tasty treats, and if you have a talent for cooking you might find yourself baking them every day!"

One of the girls looked up from decorating a cake, waving at us with a smile that seemed far too large and… suspiciously genuine.

"Cupcake?" one of the girls in the bakery asked, holding a tray in front of us.

The three of us looked at one another, and suddenly I found myself just as lost and con-fused as the other two girls. I was momentarily distracted by the sound coming from another tent. Singing?

"It's okay. Go ahead and try one!" Haley said, her enthusiasm only growing with each passing moment. She picked up one herself, peeling back the wrapper and taking a large bite. She wiped away some of the icing that smeared on her lips, licking it from her fingers. "Delicious."

There was no reason to drug us. Out here, surrounded by soldiers, escape would be difficult for a regular person. Despite some strange behavior, no one here seemed to be influenced by any kind of substance.

I picked up a cupcake and took a bite, pausing for a moment afterward to gather my thoughts.

"Wow..." I said. "These are really, really good." I hoped my disbelief didn't come across as an insult to the girls doing the baking, as I'm sure it sounded.

The other two girls followed my lead, sampling a cupcake of their own. The three of us shared another one of those looks. This was... completely unexpected. Though it made me even more cautious. Strange often did not lead to pleasant.

"Now, let's follow some of these baked treats to... the cafe!" she exclaimed, again with far more enthusiasm than seemed appropriate. We walked into another tent. Ah, so this was where the singing was coming from.

Several girls were playing instruments on stage, while one was singing softly. Haley immediately lowered her voice, as though we'd stepped into a library.

"Shh. Lila's singing right now. We don't want to interrupt the show. Let's ease over to the counter."

Several soldiers were seated, wearing casual uniform. No power suits, but that wasn't the strangest part.

"Where are the dogs and cats?" I asked in a lowered voice.

Haley's body tensed, and for a moment her enthusiasm dropped down a peg.

"Oh. That's a strange question for a new-comer to have. Sorry, I'm not the best person to answer that question."

"Who is?" I asked, not willing to let this one go just yet.

"Any of the Adversity Management person-nel on duty would probably be more than happy to answer it for you."

I nodded, but quickly realized something else. Other than Conway, I'd not seen a single other human soldier who looked to be on duty. Not since the two I'd encountered when I first arrived.

"Haley, do you mind if I take this one out of the tour?" Conway asked. "I think she has a lot of questions that won't really be relevant to the other girls."

Haley nodded. "Oh, that's unusual, but sure. I trust your judgment, Conway."

Hold on. This might have been the strangest thing I'd seen yet. Did Conway just ask her *per-mission* to pull me out of the tour? She wasn't on the ground, groveling for the forgiveness of a PanTech soldier? Haley didn't strike me as the rebellious, gutsy sort.

"Follow me, Taylor," he said, exiting the tent. Now it was just the two of us at least, and no helmet monitoring conversation. Though, we were still in a camp so I had to be careful. We'd be easily overheard.

"This place is... unusual," I said.

"Hold that thought, Taylor," he said. "You've not experienced all our camp has to offer yet."

His phrasing wasn't all that dissimilar to Haley's, but his tone told a different story. He was frustrated. He didn't want to be here. There was a deep anger in his voice, bubbling just below the surface.

"Commander Remulo! Conway reporting in, sir. I have a new addition who wishes to see you," he said, stopping just outside of the largest tent in the camp.

"Oh, Conway, how many times do I have to tell you not to be such a stick in the mud? Do come in, please, and leave all that 'sir' business at the door."

This was not the serious, gruff voice of a commander. An imposter?

"After you," Conway said, opening the entrance to the tent.

Chapter 10

If there was one thing I'd learned in my time at PanTech, it was that whole "books and covers" thing. Remulo was a large man who sat at the head of a large table. His long hair was in dreadlocks, and a large scar ran across the length of his face. He was dark-skinned, like me, with even darker hair and eyes. It was important to remember that, when it came to PanTech, the only scars a person had were the ones they chose to keep. Every physical imperfection was easily fixed by procedures that took mere minutes, or less. He wanted to look this way. As a commander, it made sense to look imposing. He wasn't the only commander to go that route. Only, it seemed to clash with his personality.

"Good day, Professor. Please, have a seat and join me for lunch. I hope nothing offended you in your tour of my camp. Oh, and thank you for taking it easy on my men near the barrier. I do hope they didn't impede you."

"Not at all," I said. He didn't appear to be hostile toward me. At least, not at the moment. It was possible the entire infiltration plan was pointless. Regardless, it was now, and acting surprised would only give him leverage.

"Thank you for your hospitality, Commander. I enjoyed the tour. I'm afraid my own impatience is to blame. I had wished to speak with you urgently."

"You honor me with your presence. What brings you here before me today? Surely you're aware of recent events. Especially considering I've heard you were a participant."

I flinched. Had I walked into a trap? I took the knife next to my plate, gripping it tightly in my fist. I might not be able to win a fight under these conditions with a commander, but I could escape and regroup. If Ghost was watching, as he often was, he could help too.

"Please, my dear, please. Remember that I also have an enhancer, so I hear your racing heart. Do not feel you are in danger here. You are my guest. No harm will befall you in my camp."

I could sense no hostility in his voice. A young woman approached me, filling my empty glass. The aroma was familiar. Cactus wine?

"Very well. I'm sure you can understand my reluctance to relax in a camp full of soldiers who I assume should want me dead."

"The loyalists, sure. We're what you'd call defectors here. It's one of humanity's finest traits. The ability to adapt to a new set of circumstances. These animal soldiers, on the other hand…"

"Before we get into that," I interrupted. "Tell me why you've brought women from the village here."

"I've brought men too," he corrected.

"I... okay, but that makes no difference. Why are you bringing them here? I'm told they don't return."

He frowned, swirling the wine in his glass before taking a sip.

"Do you think I'm like your chieftain, aiming to build some sort of harem? Hah! Ridiculous..." He chuckled, shaking his head as he did.

"Deny it, sure, but to suggest it's ridiculous? You know very well how people in power behave without a leash."

"Oooh, you can certainly be scary when you want to be, Professor. But... yes, you're right. My apologies. I'm building a sort of... town, here. You could see me as a mayor of sorts. I'm taking these people away from their hardships and offering them free and happy lives. Would you believe me if I told you that?"

Now that I had the opening for diplomacy, I needed to capitalize on it as much as possible. Perhaps this was his strategy all along. In which case... very impressive, Commander Remulo.

"If everyone is free to go, I'll offer to take them back to the village when I leave. I have no intention of forcing them one way or the other, and since you've stated that you don't either we have no problem there."

He nodded. "As you wish. But I've distracted you from your purpose here, haven't I? Please, let me know how I can be of assistance."

"Where are the cats and dogs?" I asked.

"Ah, as I alluded to earlier, they're not quite as open to change as their human counterparts. As soon as I started disregarding instructions from HQ, they stopped recognizing me as their commander. To avoid mass bloodshed, I allowed them to walk away. They have their own camp, not all that far from here. They've recognized their own leaders, despite hating one another."

I sighed. As if I needed this to get any more complicated than it already was.

"Where are *my* dogs and cats? Explorers League."

He frowned. As one of the girls approached with food, ready to serve us, he held up his hand. Understanding his desire for privacy, she walked away.

"There was a skirmish between them and the other dogs and cats. I don't need to tell you what your own people specialize in. It isn't small-scale toe-to-toe fights with geared out soldiers. In a large-scale conflict with strategy and tactics, I suspect the outcome might be different, but in a sudden fight... well, let me get to the point. Several of your dogs and cats were killed. When I did not intervene for fear of escalating conflict in the area further, they left. I don't know where they are now."

I slammed my fist down on the table.

"So, you thought it was better to have some hostile rogue unit marauding around the village, attacking *my* people, and probably worse to come?"

"Look, Professor, with all due respect… you weren't here. It's not as if it was an easy decision for me to make. I'm a commander, implanted with an enhancer and superior armor. That isn't the case for my other soldiers. All things equal, the cats and dogs are both superior to humans in a battle. I've seen what they're capable of. Especially the cats."

I waved off the explanation. He was right. I wasn't here. I was simply in denial and didn't enjoy the fact this situation was getting more and more complicated by the minute.

"There's the matter of the virus, Commander. I doubt you've heard much about it. Is that fair to say?"

"I know of the president's plans for it. That is all. Judging by your level of anxiety, I can only assume the problem has escalated on that front as well."

"Escalated? We are past the escalation, unfortunately. Guaranteed fatality. Only vaccine I had the chance to create has the side-effect of complete sterilization. Dogs and cats are life-long, contagious carriers after infection, but are completely unaffected by it otherwise. It's the primary reason I'm here. The other is to liberate each adversity zone from PanTech control, which it seems you've… at least partially accomplished already."

Silence filled the tent for several minutes as Remulo looked down at his empty plate, absorbing everything I'd told him. It was a lot to take in. After some time, he waved over the woman who had been waiting to serve us. A bowl of soup was placed in front of us, and she topped off Remulo's wine.

"I do not envy you, Professor. Not in any way. The other zones will be even worse, given their scale, and as time passes. Something I know you realize. Do you believe this mission is realistic?"

"I don't care if it's realistic," I said, taking a spoonful of my soup and following it up with a sip of cactus wine. "How realistic it is doesn't change the fact that it's necessary."

He smiled, and nodded with more enthusiasm than I was expecting.

"Of course, if there's some way we can solve the issue with the other cats and dogs diplomatically…"

"I don't care how its solved," I said. "As long as its solved. The PanTech chain of command doesn't exist anymore. I don't have any more leverage as a professor than you do as a commander. I can only ask you, as someone who clearly has a vision for a better world, to please do what you can to assist me in preserving what remains of humanity."

"Conway is on speaking terms with the animals. Perhaps he could serve as a mutual contact."

"Why is Conway on good terms with them, but not you?"

Remulo sighed again, rubbing his forehead. "They agreed strongly that we should return to HQ, but I don't think Conway realizes it's for different reasons. Or at least he didn't realize it right away, and now he's just trying to keep the peace. If you could call it peace."

"An uneasy peace is better than open war. Conway has someone he wants to rescue. That much is clear. I do too… and for that reason, I don't disagree with him. I understand your desire for peace, too. Unfortunately, I just don't think we're in a position to have it all."

Remulo nodded, his mood further darkening.

"I will think on this, Professor. The situation is certainly more dire than I realized. I might have acted differently, had I known."

"You didn't know. But now that you do, I hope you'll reconsider your position. I could use your help... and so could those who may still be trapped inside at PanTech HQ. Another commander and soldiers joining the resistance could turn the tide. Once that's over, maybe then there'll be time for peace."

"I doubt that," he said. "Perhaps I've been foolish. Would a few days to think things over and discuss it with the others be too much to ask?"

"I'll return in three days. Please have your answer by then. Humans could start dying from the virus any day now, and by the time I reach other zones who knows what kind of shape they'll be in."

"Fair enough," he said. "I will have a decision for you in three days' time."

"Commander!" Conway shouted, spilling into the tent.

"What is it? What's happening?" Remulo asked, rising quickly to his feet.

"Scouts just spotted an animal unit coming in fast. At least thirty."

"No way they'd be this brazen..." Remulo mumbled.

"Commander, your orders?" Conway shouted.

Remulo paced for a moment. Whatever he'd been hoping to avoid, it was now on the verge of crossing the point of no return.

"All soldiers are to suit up and ready their weapons. Treat this approach as an imminent attack… and pray to whatever gods you might worship that it isn't."

Chapter 11

A commotion had already begun to stir outside, as many were reacting to Conway running through the camp and some overheard his shouting inside the tent. The prospect of having to potentially fight beings you were responsible for creating was… painful, to put it mildly. I thought back to the beagle Henry, who was the first of our dogs to undergo the experiment, post-birth. He was sweet, kind, and certainly as far from dangerous as anyone could possibly conceive. I was glad, at this moment, he'd stayed with Linda instead of coming with me.

"Professor, would you come and meet them with me?" Remulo asked. "They might listen to sense from one of their creators."

I nodded. "I'll go with you, but I doubt they'll listen to anyone. It's worth a try."

Remulo placed a hand on my shoulder, then turned his attention to Conway.

"Conway, I want you to move citizens to the furthest corner of the camp. Reroute one of our scouts to watch that side. Last thing we need is to be flanked."

"Will do, Commander."

As Conway scrambled to alert and relocate the citizens, Remulo and I approached the entrance to the camp. He handed me his sidearm without comment, which I was relieved to accept.

We stood in the eerie silence for several minutes before I could start to see three vehicles approaching from the distance. They got very close before stopping, and a cat hopped out.

"Let me guess. Only cats this time, huh?" I said, causing the cat approaching us to visibly wrinkle his nose in annoyance.

I knew these cats well. Their amazing traits, and their flaws. Everyone assumed, I believed wrongly, that these cats and dogs behaved this way because of their animal nature. Instead, I theorized the answer was likely simpler than that.

The experiments leading to their creation only took place a few years prior, meaning that each one of these soldiers had been nurtured in a lab and artificially aged. They were educated with the same rapid education protocol new PanTech employees used, but lacked world experience needed to form maturity, good decision making, and a level head. All that to say they ranged anywhere from rambunctious toddlers to angsty teenagers. In adult bodies. Their species meant far less, but exacerbated certain things. Dogs tended to follow rules without question. Cats tended to believe their own thinking was flawless.

"Why would we trust the dogs to do something like this?" he said, sauntering over to us.

I didn't recognize his voice, so it wasn't the same cat from the market.

"They're superior diplomats. That's why. They have more patience and can control their tempers better."

Remulo leaned down and whispered to me. "Are you sure you should be antagonizing him?"

"Nothing is more enticing to a cat than proving they're better at something than a dog," I replied.

He nodded, even if he didn't seem quite convinced.

"I doubt that. Who is this?" the cat asked, gesturing to me.

"This is Professor Taylor. Your chief creator, if I'm not mistaken."

The cat laughed, then narrowed his eyes at me.

"Ah, the traitor. Did you expect me to treat you like a mother and ignore your crimes against the organization?"

"What organization?" I asked.

"PanTech!" he snapped.

"That old thing? Doesn't exist anymore. Time to move on."

He sneered at the comment. "For now. Unless you're assuming command of this mission,

I'm not here to speak with you. I'm here to inform Commander Remulo of his violations and deliver my terms."

"Taylor and I are sharing the command of the mission as of today, Carlo," Remulo said, crossing his arms. "And bold of you to deliver terms to your own commander. For someone who condemns traitors so easily, you should know soldiers have been forcefully retired for far less."

"Until HQ resolves our grievances against you, we'll be handling your rule-breaking ourselves. You have until the end of the day to deliver all the citizens you took from this village back to where they belong, and I will begin drafting measures to increase their adversity to make up for the ease you've brought to their lives. Something similar to what I implemented for the other village girl."

"The one named Cara?" I asked.

"I wasn't speaking to you," he hissed.

"You are speaking to me now," I said, taking a step forward. His eyes widened and a nervous grin danced across his lips.

"Maybe you need a reminder of the difference between our species," he said, raising his paw in the air.

My blood boiled. My heart raced and I could feel my body swimming in adrenaline. As bad as a cat's temper was, mine was not much better. Knowing he'd done that to Cara filled me with a raw rage. The moment he swung, I'd catch his arm and punch his head off.

Just before the cat's claws could fall, Remulo jumped between us, holding out his arms.

"Come now, leaders should never lower themselves to striking the first blow, Carlo. If we decide to fight, we'll do it properly, not skirmish outside of camp like rowdy children. We'll need a moment to discuss your terms if you'd be so kind."

Without waiting for an answer, he grabbed me by the arm and pulled me back.

"You were doing well, then you lost it. What happened?" he asked.

I sighed, rubbing my face. "My friend has been kept on the brink of death because of these idiotic adversity measures. And *you* let them happen. *You* are the commander."

His shoulders slumped. "You're letting your anger get the better of you but... you are not wrong. Should we play in to their demands for now, to buy time?"

I took a deep breath and exhaled, pulling my rage back under control. For now.

"Unfortunately, I think that will only embolden them. If you embolden them too much, they'll just casually attack you when you aren't expecting it because they will lose all respect for you as a warrior."

Remulo shook his head. "That's not really leaving me with any right answers to work with, Professor. I think the best course of action will be to go along with them for now and make plans to deal with this confrontation in a more decisive way. I'm not sure any other kind of strategy will work for us anymore."

I agreed. It had already gone beyond the point of no return without him even realizing it. Missteps had a way of devolving quickly, moving in a direction you eventually couldn't turn around from.

"That's a mistake," I said, hoping I was wrong.

"We'll agree to your demands," Remulo said, approaching Carlo. "I'll take everyone back to the village."

Carlo laughed. "I'm glad you're such a reasonable man, Remulo. Now, as for the professor there, she doesn't strike me as the type who will ever give up. She will need a bit more convincing."

He waved at the vehicle behind him. The door opened, and a large cat stepped out, yanking Cara behind him, barely able to stand on her own.

"Taylor, I'm… I'm sorry," she said.

"I'm warning you. I know what you think you're doing, but you don't know me the way you think you do," I said, speaking as calmly as I could manage.

"Surprised? We saw you entering her home. Knew you had to be friends. The rest was easy to figure out. We examined her blood this morning and found tampering that couldn't have been done by anyone other than a PanTech employee. You need to understand that you're outmatched here."

"You need to understand that you're about to cross a red line," I said.

He hesitated a moment, seeming to lose his nerve, even if just slightly.

"You talk like you're some kind of threat. Krel, kill the—"

A fist slammed into Carlo's face, so hard I thought for a moment he'd disappeared. He was knocked to the ground, rolling and bouncing across the sand like he'd landed from the sky. I personally knew how taxing that kind of display from an enhancer was, but if a show of force was needed, that would surely make an impression.

Remulo held the cat next to Cara in the air by his throat, squeezing slightly.

"This playtime is over. If you can't be reasoned with, then you've outlived—"

A cat emerged from one of the vehicles to his left, in his blind spot. I quickly reacted, aided by my own enhancer, firing before the cat could fully lift his weapon. Just this once, I aimed to wound rather than kill, striking the cat's paw. Another emerged, took one look at his friend, then me, and lowered his weapon.

Remulo would not be able to pull that same trick again without serious risk. It was time to double down. If we failed this bluff, and Remulo ended up out of commission, the human soldiers here would not win. I knew that. Remulo knew that. We could not let these cats know it.

"That's right. I'm enhanced as well. The two of us alone are plenty to rip your whole unit to shreds in seconds. You've taken advantage of your commander's kindness, but it's only because of your commander's kindness that any of you still breathe. When I said it was your final warning, I meant every word of it. Knowing that, do you still wish to disregard it? If you do, there'll be no going back. My companion has already scouted your camp, and you can all be decommissioned with the snap of my finger. I made you, and I can unmake you just as easily."

"She's... bluffing..." Carlo moaned. His helmet had been shattered, but he remained barely conscious. A feat that seemed almost impossible. Cats were truly resilient creatures.

"Find out if I'm bluffing the hard way, if that's what you prefer. It makes no difference to me," I said, holding out my fingers, ready to snap them.

The cat holding Cara released her, dropping the blaster he held in his other paw.

"We surrender!"

My head swam with the sudden rush of relief.

That was close.

Far too close.

Chapter 12

I was so far past my breaking point I could barely hold it together. But I had to. A show of weakness in this moment would unravel all our efforts and undermine Remulo's big gamble.

I walked over to Cara and picked her up in my arms, saying nothing. I stomped off toward the camp, counting backward in my head, careful not to look at anyone.

One of the soldiers rushed out of the camp. He was probably trying to assist me. I wasn't sure. I bumped into him and kept walking forward. I heard Remulo shout behind me.

"Out of her way! Give her space!"

Perhaps he understood what was going through my mind in this moment. Perhaps he didn't. None of that mattered.

"Taylor, it's okay," Cara said.

I clenched my teeth, shaking my head, blocking out her voice. Until finally I came to a small, empty tent. I took Cara inside and sat her on the floor.

I fell to my knees, burying my face into my hands. The floodgates broke away. I cried so hard I could barely breathe. It almost happened again. The image of Linus bleeding out on the desert sand flooded into every corner of my thoughts. Frelya forcing me to escape the final battle. Her goodbye to me. I couldn't do this. I wasn't some strong hero. I was just a normal woman. There was nothing special about me. I couldn't take it anymore.

I felt a weak slap hit my cheek and looked up to see Cara grabbing my shoulders. Her grip was so frail I could barely feel it.

"I can't do it, Cara. I can't do this anymore."

"I'm not the only person who needs you, Taylor. Across all the adversity zones, there are thousands just like me. If you don't save them, will anyone?"

"But why me…? Why does it have to be me? Everything I touch falls apart. People I love keep dying in my place and… I can't do it, Cara. I almost lost you too. I'm not the best person for something this big."

"You don't have to be the best person, Taylor. We don't need the best person. We need you."

I scooted closer to Cara, wrapping my arms around her and holding her close.

"Can we just sit like this for a minute?"

"Of course," she said, returning my embrace.

As my nerves began to calm, the realization finally sank in. I almost lost her, but I didn't. I tried to focus more on that than the hypothetical.

"Professor!" Conway shouted, flying through the opening of the tent. "Thank goodness I found you."

"Not now, Conway!" I snapped.

He looked at Cara and me, but was undeterred.

"I'm so sorry for my intrusion. I know it's a bad time, but it's Haley! She's collapsed and we can't figure out what's wrong with her."

No. Not yet. I needed more time. Maybe it was something else. A stress response. Maybe she got excited and fainted. Not yet.

"I'll be back," I said, releasing Cara, then looking to Conway. "Take care of her."

I jumped to my feet and scrambled from the tent.

"I will. Haley's at the commander's tent," he shouted behind me, as I realized I hadn't even asked.

I ran as fast as my feet would carry me, shoving aside the crowd as I entered the tent. Remulo was kneeling on the floor, holding her in his arms. He was frantic.

"I injected her with a stabilizer. It should've... it's like I didn't do anything at all!"

"Give me space," I said, pulling her from his arms and placing her flat on the floor. I held my ear to her chest. Her heartbeat was erratic, but extremely weak.

I took the diagnostic device from one of the hidden pockets on my dress, holding her hand and pricking her finger.

I stared at the screen for a moment, my eyes wide. The virus was fully active. It had activated.

"Hang in there!" I shouted, fumbling in my other pocket for the roll of syringes containing the vaccine. I didn't even bother sterilizing, stabbing it in her arm the moment my hand gripped it. I knew it probably wouldn't work at this stage, but I had to try.

"Is that it? Will it work?" Remulo asked, hovering over us.

I ignored him, holding my ear against her chest. I listened closely. Her heartbeat seemed to stabilize for a moment. My own heart seemed to stop, like time itself. Everything in the room froze in place as I anticipated each beat.

Then… nothing.

I immediately began CPR. Maybe if I could start her heart back.

"Remulo. Her heart!" I shouted.

He wasted no time, disappearing only briefly before returning with a small device. I moved aside as he stabbed it into her chest. We watched the data closely as it flowed across the device's screen. Several minutes passed, and it felt like hours. Remulo slowly gripped the device, removing it and cradling her in his arms.

He said nothing. There was nothing to say. I understood.

"When you're ready, come find me. We need to speak urgently."

I waved everyone else out of the tent and sat outside. I waited patiently. No doubt he was feeling responsible. But time was running out. Our window was closing. This would be the only zone in a position to catch the virus early. There would never be a better chance, or another chance at all. Not for the others.

It was rare to see a crowded place so quiet. Even the cats who briefly visited before returning to their own camp said little. They passed their information through Conway. Their plan was to return the next day with their gear and merge with the main camp, no doubt reigniting the debate about whether they should return to HQ or stay here. Things had already been complicated, but they were about to be exponentially more.

Ten minutes later, Remulo exited the tent. He came and sat down beside me, and we looked up at the sky. Neither of us said anything to the other. Just watched as the stars began to emerge.

After a while, Remulo was the one to break the silence.

"You can't see them at PanTech HQ, you know?"

"The stars?" I asked.

"Yeah... I feel like there's some metaphor buried there. Something about seeing what's right in front of you, but I can't quite articulate it in this moment."

"I need your help," I said.

He nodded. "Tell me what you need."

"I have friends working on ways to help me create more of these vaccines. Now that HQ is out of commission, and none of the labs are available anymore, we don't have an infinite number of resources to work with. I assume you have a self-sterilizing injection device here. It's one of the few things I wasn't able to get my hands on. I'll need yours, and whatever else you might have here that will help me vaccinate as many as possible."

"We should mandate vaccination immediately," he said.

I shook my head. "Under normal circumstances, that might be worth considering. You need to understand that, by this point, there likely isn't a human alive who hasn't been exposed or can avoid exposure to this virus. It's certainly the most contagious virus humanity has ever encountered, along with being the most fatal. We don't really gain anything as a group by mandating it. The consequences are individual, so the choice should be individual."

Remulo pondered a moment, and his face contorted as he did. I expected him to disagree and debate the point, but he didn't.

"I'll defer to your expertise on the matter," he said. "What else can I do for you?"

"While we won't be mandating it, I still want to make the case for the vaccine as clearly as possible and make sure we communicate it without interference. PanTech's rule is over. Useful idiots like this village's chief are no longer useful to anyone. I'd argue they never were. My father has been studying the laws here and believes he has a way to remove the chief peacefully using the laws that are already in place. I'd also like you to meet with him as soon as you're ready."

"You understand I'm going to have resistance. Reuniting with the cats and dogs is going to come at a price. They're likely to renew their call to return to HQ louder than ever. I'm not sure how they'll feel about another mission here."

"I'll speak with them tomorrow, when they arrive," I said. "I think I can convince them, now that we've regained our credibility. Respect goes a long way with them. The dogs will be easy to convince. The cats welcome an impossible challenge, and that I can certainly offer them."

"I'm going to get some rest," he said. "This is so much more than I signed up for."

"You and me both…"

Chapter 13

The next morning, I awoke to a loud argument outside my tent. Several of the voices were familiar. Some weren't.

I could overhear enough of it that I knew what it was about. Not that I couldn't have guessed anyway. I exited my tent and joined the group, deciding it best to stay quiet for now.

"Squashing the usurpers would be the quickest way to restore order, and probably the only way," Carlo hissed.

Remulo gestured toward me. "And yet we've already been informed that everyone is being seen by these machines as a usurper, no matter whether they were loyal or not. Human, cat, or dog. They are staying contained inside the walls for now. We should not provoke them to leave."

"But there are people in there who are trapped!" Conway shouted. "We are the only ones who can get them out."

"No, you're not," I said, stepping closer to the group.

"Well, that's a relief," Conway said. I wasn't sure if it was sarcasm.

"If you could track down my Explorers League units, they are specialized in taking down these machines. No offense, but they could probably destroy ten to your one."

"Is that so?" Carlo asked. "They didn't seem that tough to me."

"That's because you're a kitten," I said. "Your body's strong but you've got the brain of a two-year-old and you act like it." Remulo and Conway both shrank back as I began to scold the cats and dogs present. "How dare you attack members of my Explorers League... If you think I'll forgive that just because you've re-joined your main party, you're mistaken. That's the only thing that will keep you safe for now. Have you ever heard of the old human game *Rock, Paper, Scissors*? Some units are more ef-fective against certain enemies than others. It's not that difficult to understand."

Carlo lowered his head. I'd expected him to escalate the argument, but it seemed the fight had truly been taken out of him.

Remulo raised his hand. "We have... all made mistakes, Professor. I won't ask that you forgive me or my soldiers. As their commander, I take full responsibility for their actions. The blood of your cats and dogs are as much on my hands as theirs." He paused a moment, looking at the dogs and cats gathered. "And that's why we must atone for those mistakes, and more. We owe the professor our aid before we decide on our own task, don't you think?"

A silence fell over the group for a moment. "That's fair," Carlo said. "And…"

A dog standing beside Carlo nudged him as he stopped speaking, prompting him to complete the sentence.

"And we're sorry. For all the trouble we've caused. For the mistakes we've made."

"That might tug at your commander's heartstrings, but it doesn't do much for me," I said, shaking my head. "Let me see your actions. Then I'll see how repentant you truly are."

Carlo saluted, followed by the other dogs and cats. Conway and Remulo joined, along with the other human soldiers gathered around.

"So, does that finally settle it? We don't have time to endlessly debate everything, as you saw yesterday with Haley. Soon, you'll see that kind of death all around you. You'll help me deal with vaccine production and distribution here, transfer of power if needed, and return to HQ to aid any survivors still trapped inside."

"Any questions?" Remulo asked.

I was relieved when no one answered. Even though much of this leadership business was song and dance, one thing was absolutely true. There was no more time. We were well into borrowed time and every second we wasted we were stealing life from another adversity zone. And this one.

"Likely you have enough resources here to duplicate enough of this vaccine for the village and then some. Your lab isn't on the level of anything at HQ, but it'll suit our needs perfectly here. I'm going to give a sample to one of your most capable, and Ghost will be here shortly to aid you through the process. You're to follow his directions as if they were my own."

"Ghost?" Remulo asked. "Isn't that your falcon companion? I've not even seen him."

"He's here. Somewhere. We have comms, and he shows up when he's most needed. Otherwise, you'll never see him. Name suits him, right?"

Everyone looked between one another, like I'd lost my mind, but no one questioned.

"Conway, are you up for it?" Remulo asked.

He nodded, holding out his hand to receive one of the vaccine syringes. I gave him two, so he'd have an extra in case something went wrong.

"Animals are carriers for this virus, but do not show symptoms. There's nothing I can do about that. For humans, this vaccine does not prevent or destroy the virus. It only prevents it from activating and killing the host, with the side-effect of sterilization. It will spread no matter what we do. Given every PanTech employee is already sterilized there's no reason for you not to get it. Still, it's your choice. For you villagers present, make sure you choose carefully. The virus can sometimes take years to activate. You could have a child, maybe two, and allow them to be vaccinated. This is your choice. Whoever is ready to be vaccinated now, please line up at the table in the commander's tent."

I began walking toward the tent, and most of the humans in the gathering followed. I wouldn't have enough syringes to vaccinate them all.

Suddenly, a dark blur shot in front of me, coming to a stop with a few hops on the sand.

"Your timing is perfect, Ghost."

Without comment, he released a bag from his talon, sliding it toward me. I picked it up, opened it and... more vaccines. World's best partner. Sometimes.

"You really are the best, Ghost. Though maybe you could've shown up yesterday."

"Always nitpicking..." Ghost said. "You had it under control. This was more important. I've also been scouting for the lost Explorers League unit."

"And?" I asked. I couldn't help but feel a surge of hope.

"Traces, but nothing yet. They are skilled at covering their tracks."

I nodded. "Please help Conway with creating more vaccines. Once he has the hang of it, resume your search."

No acknowledgment. He just flew off.

"Was that...?" one of the village girls asked, her eyes wide in disbelief. "Was that a shadowfalcon?"

"It was. The first and last one I've ever seen. But as excited as many of you probably are to find out a shadowfalcon is real, we have more important things to do right now. Save the shadowfalcon Q&A for another time."

She frowned, but kept walking behind me.

Entering the tent, I saw Cara sitting at a small table, a smile on her face and an empty chair beside her. Two other empty chairs at either side.

"Shouldn't you be resting?" I asked.

"Shouldn't you? I'm feeling great," she said.

I wasn't going to argue with her. She certainly looked better than she had since I returned. Now her health could be restored more rapidly, without fear of discovery or punishment.

"Fair enough. Are you ready to get started then? We'll split the line. Upper arm is fine."

Cara nodded. "Okay, everyone, please split into two lines and we'll take care of you."

Within seconds, a nice clean, even line formed. I breathed a sigh of relief. This probably wouldn't go as smoothly in the village. Still, it was a great trial run.

One after another, we vaccinated the group. Several dozen. I had plenty of vaccines to spare, but nowhere near enough for the entire village.

A few of the young women had watched from the sidelines, nervously contemplating.

"Are you sure you don't want to do this now?" I asked.

They looked at each other, and one shook her head. "No. I think I want to wait. Can you get it when you're pregnant?"

I nodded. "Yes. If you want to get pregnant first, you can get the vaccine while you're pregnant. But that isn't enough to protect your child. They'll need to be vaccinated too. And... well, I want to be completely honest with you. There are some situations where we haven't observed this virus in action. We don't know if it can attack a child in the womb or if the mother being vaccinated has any effect on that. There are a lot of things we just don't know. I'm sorry. I wish I could give you all the information so you could be more confident in your decision."

"No... thank you, Professor, err, Taylor. Thank you for coming back to help us. It's caused you a lot of trouble."

I laughed. Not because it was funny, but because I knew this would probably be the easiest adversity zone to deal with. It would only get worse, and much, much more complicated from here.

"You're welcome," I said.

For the first time since I came back, I finally felt like I was making a difference.

Chapter 14

If there was one thing that could always be counted on from my father, it was that he was stubborn. Kind, wise, but stubborn above everything else. So much so that it was the first thing Mother warned anyone about when they wanted to get to know him. Being his only daughter, I was always given a bit of favoritism, despite the fact such favoritism was strictly forbidden. Father didn't care. He never followed PanTech's rules, or direction, and of all the people in this village, they disliked him the most. His inventions threatened to advance the village out of its technology classification, to the point he was banned from continuing his work. I knew he would not be easy to convince about PanTech's involvement.

I didn't realize he'd be *this* difficult.

"Are you sure?" I asked. "He's refusing to come and meet with us?"

"Yes, Professor," Conway said.

"Like… completely refusing?"

Conway sighed. "I suppose we could force him to come, but that would defeat the purpose."

"I'll go speak to him," I said.

I really didn't have time for this, but I needed to hear him out.

I let Ghost and the others know I'd be away, and returned to the village.

**

Entering our home, I walked into a room filled with smoke and Father, somehow, reading a book upon a pile of books through the haze.

"Ah, Taylor. Welcome back."

"I love you. You know that, right?"

"I love you, too, but I see that you are quite angry with me. Here. Sit. Smoke a pipe with me," he said.

"Mother will have a conniption," I said, laughing as I lit the other pipe. I had been expected.

I took a puff. It had been a while since I'd tried one. I attempted, clumsily, to blow a ring, prompting a laugh from Father.

"Your mother will be alright. I'm afraid in my fixation on my work I've smoked her out of the house entirely, and quite literally."

"Please don't tell me you were too busy to answer my request. I know what you're studying is important, but it isn't more important than the issue at hand."

Father closed the book in front of him and sighed.

"I'm afraid I must disagree with you there, even though you are not wrong."

"Aren't you contradicting yourself, then?" I asked.

"If whatever we establish in this village is to last, it must be achieved without PanTech's intervention. Offer your vaccine, sure, but I will not agree to the current chieftain being removed by force."

"It's expediting the process. We both know that's exactly how things will end. The villagers have no loyalty to the chieftain. Everyone here hates him. They'll cheer when he's removed. I know you aren't doing this for the recognition, or the fame, or because you think you'll be the best for the job. I know you. You're one of the few people, probably in history, who actually wants to lead for the right reasons. But you could put a pig up against the chieftain, and it would win."

"That isn't the point," he said, puffing on his pipe, blowing several perfect rings. Show off.

"Enlighten me."

"It's the precedent that establishes. Even if we only have a couple of generations left, I am not a young man. Power is likely to pass several more times before all is said and done. Do you want to establish this new era by allowing the greatest show of force to dictate who should lead? And for PanTech to deliver that force, of all people?"

I pondered his words for a moment. I was in a hurry. This was wasting precious time. And yet... he wasn't wrong. My eagerness to finish matters here and move on was pushing me to take shortcuts.

"How might we compromise?" I asked. "I cannot afford to delay vaccinating the villagers for weeks or months of political process. I won't call it pointless, but delaying me even days could cause the deaths of thousands."

"Yes... you are right. That is why I have amended the plan and will... stretch the law a bit to accommodate the circumstances. I will ask, with the backing of the villagers, that the chief recognizes the need for an emergency election due to the crisis we are facing. If the ruling party—which we can fairly say is Pan-Tech—is abandoning their rule, then an election must take place. Even if he does not officially claim to represent them, it is common knowledge that he is their representative."

"And if he refuses?" I asked.

"A rhetorical question, is it not?"

"I'm sorry to be the villain here, Father, but I simply can't choose to go about things in the optimal way if that means spending more time at the cost of an untold number of lives. Every day, hour, or minute I waste is precious. I'm only human, so I'm never going to be running at maximum efficiency, but I have to make the best time where I can."

He smiled. "You aren't the villain, Taylor. You are the savior of this village, and in all the ways that matter, humanity itself. No matter how much I disagree with certain things, that fact will remain. However…"

"I was waiting for that," I said.

"That doesn't mean we'll always agree about everything."

I nodded. "Of course not. You didn't raise me to blindly follow rules or respect authority where it hasn't been earned. Yet, here I am in the position of authority, making demands. And, even knowing that, I must continue to do so."

"Very well. Do you represent the PanTech employees present?"

"Depends, but for the most part, yes. I can speak for them."

"Then I'd like you to help me draft this declaration, formally dissolving PanTech's authority as a ruling body, and relinquishing that control to the village itself."

"Father, if I do that, and he uses some kind of underhanded tactic to preserve his position, what then?"

"Then we will have lost anyway. Without PanTech's support, things that often happen in history will happen here."

I raised a brow. "You're referring to an uprising? A violent overthrow? So why even bother with all of this theater in between? Let's just drag him out by the hair and be done with him!"

"It's the chance, Taylor. The chance that things might transition properly and set a precedent for all future leaders to be restrained by. A standard to be held to."

"Fine, but the deal is I'm only waiting to see how your plan plays out. If we aren't allowed to intervene, there's no point in delaying my departure. I'll see that these terms are honored, wait for the emergency election to conclude, and administer the vaccine to those who desire it. You could have villagers vote on mandating at the same time, since that will be out of our hands if we relinquish control, but I'm personally against it. The acting commander of this zone, Remulo, is in favor of it. Suppose that'll be something for you to sort out."

"I am also against it. Though I'm sure you aren't surprised by that," he said.

"Given the way the virus and the vaccine work, not really. The usual debates around mandating aren't really applicable here."

"Isn't it amazing that we are still having those same debates hundreds, sometimes thousands of years later?"

"That's because value systems change, revert, and change again," I said.

He grinned.

"Oh, don't get me wrong. I know why. I just find it fascinating."

"I find it depressing," I said. "That all we could manage to do is turn in circles and chase our tails for thousands of years. Technology changed. Lots of things changed. Except the core of our thinking. It never really evolved."

"Such a cynical way of viewing the world, Taylor. Just because we observe things to be a certain way, doesn't mean we should close ourselves off to the exceptions. It's these small, isolated moments where we choose to go against that established way that inch humanity forward."

"Toward oblivion," I said, trying and failing again to blow a smoke circle.

"When one has nothing to lose, doing the right thing does not become less important. It is, in those moments, where it becomes more important than ever."

"Thank you," I said. "For everything you've done for me. When all of this is over, I don't know if I'll ever see you again. I just wanted to say… thank you for everything."

He reached out, squeezing my hand. "My daughter, wisdom has not only passed one way. I feel I have learned from you as well. I should also thank you."

"Let's draft this document, then. I don't need to cry any more than I already have these past few days."

He smiled a warm smile. "Alright, but then I must teach you how to blow a smoke ring properly. It'll only take a few minutes, and you can practice it later."

"Deal."

Chapter 15

We spent hours working. I hadn't realized just how long it had been since I'd spent time writing by hand. What a strange feeling it was. The slow, physical effort needed to say a word almost gave them more weight. Perhaps it did. I couldn't simply think the words, as I could at PanTech, and suddenly have them transcribed. My hand gripped the quill, and it was like I slowly fell back in time, and part of me reverted to times past. Father was patient with my clumsiness, believing in me as he always did to see the task through, which I did.

"I believe my section is finished. Whenever you're ready, we'll exchange and look them over," he said.

Even though my section was about half the length of his, it had taken me twice as long to draft, even with Father's notes already spread across the table around me. Mother had returned, relieved to see the smoke had cleared and happy to see me. Though, she didn't disturb us. She fetched us drinks and snacks silently. She'd long since grown accustomed to Father's long bouts of fixation on his work. Were it not for her, he might've starved or died of thirst during one of them. He wouldn't eat or drink until the task was finished, and it seemed I'd inherited the curse.

As I scribbled the final marks on the page, I handed it to Father, taking his in exchange and reading over it, comparing it to the mountain of legal notes he'd taken. Even understanding his motivation, this all felt so pointless. It felt like a child holding an elaborate political election for his action figures, but perhaps that's simply how out of touch I'd grown in just a few short years. Now that certain options were available to me, I had difficulty seeing others. I had changed. I feared not for the better.

"Two small errors on the second page. I suggest rewording the last paragraph on the third page for clarity," I said.

Father nodded, reviewing the work himself, then setting it aside for the corrections.

"No error in yours, though your handwriting has suffered. However, I appreciate this is a meaningless skill in the world you've lived in these past years."

"I was just reflecting on that. At PanTech, there was an onboarding period of several months dedicated completely to prying people away from their old ways of doing things and into the new. Writing with your thoughts is certainly easier."

Father laughed. "There were those who resisted such advancements? I'll tell you for certain that I'd switch to such a system tomorrow if it were offered to me."

"You're an inventor and scholar," I said. "Even though everyone at PanTech was highly intelligent, some of them were more traditional and believed making things easier sometimes cheapened the quality of the output. Like how deliberate we had to be with this ink on paper. Correcting errors isn't as easy as a thought."

Father waved his hand, relighting his pipe and taking a puff.

"That's nonsense," he said. "Mostly."

"Are you looking forward to confronting the chieftain? I certainly am," I said.

"So am I, though likely for different reasons than you. You are hoping he will do something foolish, but I only caution you against doing something foolish yourself."

"I will try," I said.

***

In truth, this was less of a traditional village and more like a mini dictatorship. One man, placed in the seat of power as a puppet, with no system of checks and balances. The laws Father studied were nothing more than a farce, cobbled together by PanTech to give the illusion of legitimacy. They weren't meant to be scrutinized or questioned, and they certainly weren't meant for the chieftain to follow. He and his were above the law. Just like those who came before him, he was handpicked by PanTech's Adversity Management for his willingness to do whatever he was told in exchange for being able to do whatever he wanted otherwise.

In a normal society, a man like him would've been dragged out and beheaded in the streets. A long time ago. Instead, armed super soldiers protected him from any opposition or criticism.

I decided it best to bring Father to meet with Commander Remulo and the others anyway, and to offer Remulo the option of being present when the documents were delivered.

To my surprise, Father and Remulo hit it off almost immediately, smoking and chatting.

Father had made a more charismatic statesman than I ever expected to see. Strange to me, knowing that internally he despised it all.

Remulo finally finished reading over the documents, placing them on the table in front of him.

"I have my reservations, though I'm sure you two have already discussed them. If we are approaching this agreement in good faith, we will not be able to step in and replace the village chieftain, nor will we be able to enforce any kind of peaceful transition. I'm sure you realize the chieftain, being able to offer virtually unlimited favors, has other villagers under his thumb. It might even surprise you to know how far his influence webs throughout the village. Despite the man being… the way he is… he is competent at networking and building dependence on his favors."

"Much of this will crumble once PanTech removes their support and relinquishes its right to govern," Father said.

"I am concerned about another thing," Remulo said, his expression darkening. "If any well-known PanTech employee—present *or* past—interferes in this process, it will undermine the legitimacy. Anyone can look at it and say Pan-Tech is being dishonest and will not relinquish control. They will assume the whole thing is a farce and that we were placing another leader there from the shadows. It will be no different from us just doing it directly. And frankly, much more quickly."

"This was the point I tried to make with him," I said.

"You do understand what this means, correct? Not only will I not be able to protect you, but Taylor—as a former PanTech professor—will not be able to protect you. Your wife—a former PanTech Adversity Management commander—will not be able to help you. I've done my homework on you. You are an honest man, and a scholar. Taylor and your wife could likely protect you from threats, but without them? If I may be so bold, I believe the appropriate expression would be to say you are a sitting duck."

"Except I'm PanTech's most despised traitor at the moment. Would I not be an exception?" I asked.

Father shook his head. "All the more reason you can't interfere, Taylor. Your own motivations are very clear, even more than anyone else. I will simply have to take the risk. I will seek protection from those who reside in the village. There should be no shortage of volunteers, given the chief's reputation."

"And no shortage of those who could come after you, because of that very same reputation," Remulo said.

"I really am afraid for you, Father. I don't want to see you get hurt or worse, no matter how important this is," I said, fighting back my emotions as best I could. I had not been so direct about it before, but it had weighed heavily on me throughout the entire discussion.

"I understand, Taylor. Your mother has said the same thing. Though, as she has pointed out, she has not been associated with PanTech for over twenty years. Most of the villagers aren't even aware she was ever with them at all. Although neither of us are as young as we used to be, I trust your mother to handle my protection."

Remulo dropped his elbows on the table, locked his fingers, and rested his chin, sighing loudly.

"There really aren't any good choices for anything anymore. Every day is deciding between which bad choice is worse, then going with the other. I fear that's all we have left. I will leave the choice of our side of things to Taylor. We are hard at work preparing the necessary vaccinations and repairing discord in our own ranks. In truth, all of that considered, staying out of things is for the best."

Remulo took up the quill Father brought along, dipped it in ink, and stared at it for a moment. After hesitating, he scribbled his signature across the bottom.

"Thank you," Father said.

"Please... do not thank me yet. You may be cursing this decision before all is said and done."

"This leaves confronting the chieftain," I said. "As a representative of PanTech, I will be at the forefront of this process until the chieftain accepts PanTech's withdrawal and agrees to an emergency election. After that..."

Father shook his head.

"Convincing him likely will not be easy, so it will be good to have your help, Taylor. After that, I only ask that you put your faith in me and do not blame yourself, regardless of the outcome. This is my choice, and I will bear the burden of the consequences."

"Saying that will not make those consequences any easier to bear," I said.

"Are you ready to present these documents to the chieftain?" he asked.

"As ready as I'll ever be."

Chapter 16

I felt a sense of dread as Father and I passed through our village. As much as I hated drawing attention to myself, it was a great strategy in this case.

"Village meeting in front of the chieftain's home!" Father shouted. "Attend and make your voices heard!" He repeated this over and over, and soon we had a crowd following behind us, eager to see what all the commotion was about.

When we reached the chieftain's house, Father knocked and took a step back.

After a moment, the chieftain opened the door. To his credit, he wasn't intimidated by the gathered crowd. It was as though he'd expected us. "Ah, what have we here uh? Lot of people for a casual stroll. How can your chieftain help you today uh?"

Father walked up calmly, offering the chieftain the small stack of documents we'd prepared.

"Would you like me to summarize the contents of those documents for you?" he asked.

The chieftain grinned. "You may be a teacher, but I can indeed read uh. Just a moment." He scanned each page slowly, chuckling every so often.

"What are your thoughts?" Father asked.

"Very well researched and incredibly thorough, just as I would expect from you. However, I'm afraid I simply cannot agree to the terms uh."

"I understand," Father said. "That's fine."

"It's… fine?" the chieftain asked.

"Certainly. By not signing it you are not protected by the terms, which is your personal choice."

"I see, so this is more a threat than anything else uh."

Whispers were exchanged among those gathered, unsure of what they were witnessing, but feeling the rising tension all the same.

"If PanTech is pulling out of our village, it is certainly grounds for a special election. That fact alone. That's not even considering the virus, which is arguably an even bigger threat. In accordance with our laws, you are bound to agreement."

The chieftain laughed, shaking his head, as if being lectured by a child. "Our laws? You are a brilliant man. You know as well as I do these laws are merely for show. I was appointed to my position, as was the chieftain before me, the chieftain before him, and so on. There has never been an election in this village and there is no need. I will continue to govern after they leave just as I always have. I have no association with PanTech whatsoever uh."

"That's a lie," a woman in the crowd shouted.

"At least be honest about it," another man agreed.

"I have lived in this village since I was born. I have always lived here, and I have never worked for PanTech. Yet you accuse me of being one of them? Ridiculous. If you'd make such a claim, show proof of it."

Silence fell over the crowd. I sighed. It sounded like a powerful statement on the surface, but how could one go about proving such a thing anyway? It's not like villagers had access to PanTech employment records.

"Then you'll appreciate the need for a special election," Father said.

"First of all, this virus is a farce cooked up by your daughter. Or if it is not a farce, perhaps she has brought it here. Eh? A convenient time for you to grab power for yourself."

"I represent PanTech. My intention was to drag you out of here kicking and screaming, then feed you to the creatures of the desert. If you'd still prefer things to go that way, just let me know. I can arrange it," I said.

"Ah, see the true colors of the little witch. You? Represent PanTech? Hah! Don't make me laugh uh! You are a traitor. Did you think I would not find out about it?"

"Your information must be limited, or maybe you missed Commander Remulo's signature right in front of your face. We are pulling out, and you'll be on your own. What we do before we leave is entirely up to you."

"Commander Remulo is not the leader of PanTech uh," he said.

I laughed. "Do you really think the president is going to come all the way to your tiny little village and stand up for you? Like you're someone that actually matters? Give me a break. Sorry, Father, we tried to do things your way but I'm not wasting more time on this slimy worm if this is the way he's going to be."

I stepped forward, grabbing him by the collar of his robe. The way he smiled, like he genuinely didn't think I'd touch him...

I punched him in the face, breaking his nose. Blood poured out, dripping on the sand below. I grabbed his hair and yanked him to the ground, dragging him behind me. Father grabbed me, but I easily shrugged off his grip.

"People are *dying* while you play games! I've had enough of you."

He struggled to his knees, trying to pull his hair out of my grip. A handful separated from his scalp, freeing him temporarily.

"Help me! She's gone insane. Someone stop her!"

"No one here can stop me," I said, stepping on the back of his leg and pinning him in place. "The virus is real. It's going to kill everyone. *Everyone!*"

"Taylor…" Father pleaded, putting a hand on my shoulder. "Look around you," he said, nodding toward the crowd.

Everyone's mouth was agape in horror. If anything, I'd expected them to be cheering. This man had been nothing but awful, the truest, lowest scum of the earth and yet…

They didn't understand the virus. They hadn't seen what I'd seen. They probably weren't even fully aware of what the chieftain did in their own village. And yet, Father had *faith* in these people?

These people… they were *my* people too. In my mind, I was beginning to sound more and more like a PanTech propagandist. The greater good. Deciding what's good for a person, ignoring their own will. In my quest to liberate humanity from PanTech I'd… become them.

"I signed it!" the chieftain shouted. "It said in the document if I signed you would not interfere in the election. That is what you swore to here!"

Sure enough, he'd scribbled his signature while I was distracted.

I drew back my fist. People were dying.

Someone already died.

This filth wasn't worth wasting precious time on.

"Taylor…" Father whispered. "You aren't like them. We can be better."

I clenched my teeth. I didn't know what to do.

I moved my foot, allowing him to crawl away.

There was silence all around. All I could hear was the chieftain's pathetic wheezing as he struggled to catch his breath.

I hung my head, walking away quietly. I kept walking until I was out of the village and sat on a rock in the blazing sun. I squinted, looking out on the empty sand. I was the hero, wasn't I?

Ghost landed next to me. I was no longer surprised when this happened.

"Are you alright, Taylor?" he asked.

"We're the good guys, right?"

"You would've been correct in killing him. It would've been a kindness he's unworthy of, and saved us valuable time."

I sighed, but managed to force a smile.

"Ghost… humans are complicated."

"Unfortunately, I'll have to take your Father's side here," Mother said, suddenly appearing behind me.

I jumped.

"You could've warned me she was coming up behind us, Ghost."

Ghost stared blankly. "Why? Your mother had no intention of harming you."

I laughed. "This is why we make such great partners."

Ghost tilted his head. "That makes no sense."

As Mother sat next to me, Ghost flew off. Without a word, of course.

"Would you want to live in a world where regular people cheered an execution in the streets?" she asked.

"We aren't going to have a world left to speculate about for much longer. These moral questions are starting to blend together. I must save as many people as I can. At any cost."

"There is always a cost that's too high," she said.

"I'm not so sure."

"You spent a lot of time hearing your father out. You walked away just now, instead of killing a man who arguably deserved it."

"Ghost said it would have been too good for him," I said, as if Ghost were here to agree with me.

Mother smiled.

"Both things can be true at the same time."

"It should've been someone else," I said.

"What do you mean?" she asked, resting her hand on my back.

"It should be someone else here, fixing everything. Someone mentally stable, who always knows the right thing to do. Someone emotionally and physically strong. Someone... better."

Mother slid her arm over my shoulder, pulling me close and resting her head against mine. "You'll always feel that way, you know. You'll always ask yourself those questions. All that matters is that you keep moving ahead. When this perfect hero shows up, you can hand the torch to them. Until they do, it's you. You're going to make mistakes along the way. You're going to stumble, and fall, and feel like the villain. Sometimes you may have to be the villain. That's the burden everyone carries with a mission like yours."

"You're right, Mother. Thank you... Still, I will keep trying to be better."

"Promise me that no matter what happens with this election business over the next few days, that you'll let me handle it."

"Sure," I said, waving off the remark.

"I'm serious. I want you to promise me."

"I promise," I said.

Chapter 17

Even though I couldn't participate, Father and Mother were kind enough to keep me informed of everything going on with the upcoming election. Three days was the final agreement, down from one week. Seems the chieftain wanted me out of the village as quickly as possible. Good. For once, we wanted the same thing.

As I walked through the desert toward the Adversity Management camp, Ghost flew in and perched on my shoulder.

"How do you do, Ghost?" I asked.

He tilted his head.

"I'm fine. I came to update you about the Explorers League. I keep finding traces of them, but by the time I track them to a new location, they've already moved again. They're clever, that's for certain."

"At least things have settled down enough that we won't need them to complete the mission. You won't need to make finding them a priority anymore, though we should keep looking when we can. For now, let's focus on vaccine production and getting ready to roll out of here."

"Why didn't you use our lab for vaccine production? It's more suited to the task."

"I have trust issues, Ghost. Besides, our resources need to be preserved as much as possible."

"Aren't we returning to the survivor camp outside of HQ after this?"

"Not if we don't need to restock on supplies. They need to keep as many as they can too. They could be attacked any day... if they haven't been already."

"Are you afraid that if they're attacked, we won't have any way to replenish our resources to keep producing the vaccine?"

I stopped and sighed.

"No, Ghost, I'm not afraid of it. I know it. Unfortunately, there are too many things trying to cook us from all sides. If it was reasonable to get back in there and retake the HQ, that's what we'd be focusing on."

"Do you think they can rescue those inside?"

"No. I don't."

"Why don't you tell them that?" he asked.

"Because humans are complicated, Ghost. Commander Remulo likely understands how difficult it is just as well as I do. So does Conway and the others."

"So, why do it? Why not focus on tasks that are possible?"

"Humanity would've never made it this far if we did that."

"That makes no sense."

"I agree."

Ghost tilted his head again.

"Conway sent me to tell you that he's having trouble with repurposing one of the systems and had to halt production for now."

"When were you going to tell me this, Ghost?" I asked.

"You're already heading to the camp."

I sighed. "Your logic hurts me sometimes, Ghost. I'd still like to be mentally prepared for what I'm walking into."

"How does it hurt you?"

"I don't mean literally."

"Yes, but I still don't understand how logic hurts you. It's not like you can solve the problem from here."

"It helps with anxiety. Do you feel anxiety, Ghost?"

Ghost silently pondered for a moment, making me question whether he knew what anxiety even was.

"Occasionally," he finally said. "But likely not the same as you."

"It's why we make such good partners, Ghost. We complement each other well. It's always good to have a level-headed falcon when you're a mess of a person like me."

"You do not give yourself enough credit," Ghost said bluntly. A compliment from Ghost?

"Go and let Conway know I'm on my way," I said. "And thank you."

Ghost flew away in the direction of the camp, and my thoughts returned to the lost Explorers League unit.

Perhaps lost wasn't the right way to see them. They were clearly hanging around the area. Is it possible the machines have already broken out of HQ and are attacking zones?

Ghost made a good point. Maybe it would be best if we checked in with the survivor camp before moving on to the next zone.

The thoughts continued to swirl in my mind as I walked for hours in the desert heat, finally making my way into the camp.

"What took you so long?" Conway shouted as I came into view.

"Shut up," I said, grinning as I caught my breath. "Just tell me what the problem is."

"Better I show you," he said, leading me to the tent where he was working. Several boxes of vaccines were already sitting on a table.

"Are those okay?" I asked.

"Yes… well… yes, I think so."

"You need to know so," I scolded.

"I'm not the scientist. Ghost approved them, if that matters."

"Of course that matters!" I said. Ghost was probably smarter than both of us put together.

"Right. Yeah, you're right. That's just tough to get used to. You know, following orders from a bird."

"I'm relieved to know you're getting used to it. This is probably already enough for the village, so what's the issue?"

"Ghost said overproduction was not an issue, but that I would need to convert some of the resources to make it work. I'm not sure I'm doing it right, so Ghost suggested we bring you in for the final call."

"Ghost was being polite to you, but you're wasting my time. Did he tell you I was coming?"

"He did. Then left again…"

Conway was clearly frustrated, and I knew it would take a bit of digging. Though, probably not much. Already had a feeling.

"He wouldn't have done that if he didn't trust you were capable of completing the task with the instructions you were already given. Ghost may be a bird, but when I said to follow his directions as though they were mine I didn't mean that in some other way. It was a literal statement."

"Yeah, but… Okay… you're right," he said, sighing. He immediately pulled up the interface and began making changes.

"The animals have their moments, I know, but we created them and now our role is to help them grow. Like it or not, they will be our successors."

"If I might be so bold, Professor, that's what I worry about."

"Be clear about what you mean, Conway. I don't like playing word games and it's not like I would punish you for disagreeing with me."

"These dogs and cats are in a position where they benefit from our demise. Right now, humans control them. You might see it as teaching, but they see it differently. At least, ours did. They don't like being on a leash. They see the world differently, and they don't appreciate us forcing our way of thinking on them. All the commanders are human. Ghost is the first animal I've met who might've arguably been able to give orders to a human and even then… I find myself resenting it. In my mind, I'm wondering who he thinks he is, ordering me around like this. He's an animal, and I'm a human. That's stupid, right? But I'll bet a lot of them think the same way."

Ah, so this was the real reason Ghost wanted me to come and talk to him. No doubt he sensed this and wasn't sure how to handle it.

"So, you think they may try to sabotage us to get us out of the picture as soon as possible?"

"I know… I'm sure that makes me sound like an awful person," he said, frowning.

"No. I think that's a reasonable thing to be concerned about. I'd be lying if I said the thought hasn't crossed my mind as well. I'm sure there will be times when a cat or dog sees things that way. However, if they care about the world they're going to inherit, it would be in their best interest to help us clean up the mess as much as possible before they're left with... whatever remains."

I mostly believed what I was saying. Then again, I was cynical enough that I was probably never the right person to come to for a pep talk.

"Yes, that's a fair point," he said. His flat tone indicated he wasn't entirely convinced.

I trusted Ghost. I trusted my closest friends in the Explorers League, like Kelin. And... Harlow.

"When I escaped, it was only because of a few others. I was in the president's office when everything went down. Confronting him, face-to-face. With Frelya. She was the first reason... She ejected me from the elevator—didn't give me the choice to stay and fight with her. After that, we were pursued by dozens of machines. A cat, Kelin, was with us. She also killed the person behind the virus spreading. It was already too late, but she kept him from doing more harm. In our escape, one of the weapons we were counting on malfunctioned. A dog, Harlow... he climbed into the middle of the fray. Took shot after shot from machine guns and kept climbing. A piece was stuck in our weapon, and he fixed it. If he hadn't done that..."

I found myself getting emotional, just recalling it. Recounting it to another person made it even more difficult. I could see his face clearly in my mind. The way everyone gathered around and saluted his corpse afterward.

Conway took a deep breath and exhaled.

"I'm sorry, Taylor. You headed up the Explorers League and you worked with more dogs and cats than the rest of us combined. I appreciate your perspective. How do you do it, by the way? How do you keep going? Every day that passes, all I can think about is my older sister. She was a scientist. She didn't make it out. I don't know if she's alive, dead... I don't know if I'll ever see her again, or find her body for closure. I don't know what she's going through right now or what her last moments were like. And I can't expect the world to stop turning for my big sister but... it has for me. She's all I had left. Our parents died before we passed our exams and went to PanTech. Our whole lives, we were only separated for a few years, just long enough for me to reach the exam age."

"My little brother is out there somewhere too," I said. "Part of me hoped I would see him here, but I can only hope he's out there somewhere, like you are, overseeing one of the Adversity Zones and probably thinking about me the same way you're thinking about your sister."

"I hope he finds you one day," he said. "I feel for him."

I put a hand on his shoulder.

"I get it, Conway. You're not a bad guy for worrying about being stabbed in the back, or being afraid cats and dogs are out to get you. It isn't paranoid, and you're not crazy. It's the world we live in now. But... try to find things to hold on to. You asked me how I do it. I don't know the answer to that. I just do. Learn to rely on others as much as you can. It won't always work out, but the alternative isn't sustainable. Not with what we're trying to accomplish. It's too much for one person."

His discomfort became clearer, and he seemed eager to change the subject. It would take more time than we had to get him to fully open up.

"Done!" he said, closing the interface, forcing a smile. "Resuming production. Should be able to get a few thousand more units out of this run, but I think that's the limit of what we're going to be able to do here. I hope it's enough."

"Enough for now. Thank you, Conway. I'm going to head back to the village to keep an eye on things there. Their election's coming up soon and we'll finally be able to wrap things up here and move on."

"Looking forward to it," he said.

"Fingers crossed things actually go smoothly for once," I said.

He held up his fingers and crossed them, and I did the same.

Please let this actually go smoothly.

Chapter 18

I pressed the start button on my motorcycle, eliciting a low hum and some rattling. The rattling wasn't supposed to be there. I'd have to check that later. Becoming a mechanic was not on my bucket list, but when I found this old thing abandoned, something inside me just had to save it. I wasn't sure what era it was from, but it weathered the elements exceptionally well. It had a classic look and reminded me of some of the old world vehicles I learned about in the history archives. It was appealing. I slipped my helmet on and rolled only a few feet before Ghost nearly made me jump from my seat.

"Taylor! Can you hear me?"

On comms? Ghost had never contacted me on comms before. In fact, most of the time, I forgot we even had them. It was little more than a glorified spying device Ghost could use to know what I was up to. He hated speaking on them. This was, of course, terrifying that he was speaking to me that way now.

"I can hear you, Ghost. What is it? What's wrong?"

"I found the Explorers League unit."

"That's great. We can make contact and—"

"They are heading straight for the Adversity Management camp. They're riding to battle, and they look prepared. There's an arachnid unit with them."

"Wait. They've repurposed an arachnid machine? That means..."

"Listen!" Ghost shouted into the comm. Another first for Ghost.

"A group of men are on their way to your home. They are after your father. Two Adversity Management soldiers are with them."

"I can't be in both places at once. I'm all the way outside the barrier right now!"

"You're the only one who could talk down the Explorers League unit. If they aren't stopped, it could compromise our vaccine supply and potentially wipe out both units."

"I have to save Father."

"Listen to me. You—"

"I can't let my parents die. If that happens..."

"Taylor, I need you to trust me. Can you do that?"

I froze. Could I? We were running out of time. It was entirely possible I'd be too late no matter how fast and no matter which direction I decided to go. Why did these two things have to happen at the exact same time, and why was I so stupid to leave Twisted Key behind in my room?

"Okay. Okay! Just hurry," I said.

"Go to the Adversity Management camp. You won't make it in time to prevent the fight, but you can stop it."

I leaned forward on the bike, maxing the acceleration. I've never driven this thing that fast before, but now was as good a time as any to see what it was capable of.

The flat desert became nothing more than a tan haze. I found it difficult to breathe, but the danger felt exciting. If I made one wrong move, struck an obstacle, anything, I'd likely be dead. Nothing about that should be exciting to a normal person, but at this point, I suppose it had become yet another coping mechanism.

As the Adversity Management camp came into sight, I could already hear fighting. The familiar whizzes and whirs of the arachnid unit grated against my mind like the sand itself. It was the first thing that came into sight.

It stood the height of a small house. Menacing red lights darted about, seeking prey. The body itself was deceptively small, but extremely difficult to reach through its long, sharp, and nimble legs. Machine guns were mounted to either side of the processing unit in the center, heavily armored by extremely thick, tempered-glass-like material. Most of the old units encountered in the wild—before the president started manufacturing new ones—were barely functional and had long since run empty on ammunition. A refurbished unit, stocked on ammo and fully functional was a nightmarish thing to behold. To think they'd reprogram one to use on their own people…

The shouting was indistinguishable. I didn't see Ghost, but I trusted him. I had to trust him.

I focused all my attention on the machine. It had to go down first. We'd experimented with controlling them in the past, and I knew how volatile that was. Internally, they'd often remap controls in a matter of hours and become fully autonomous and hostile again. I doubted they'd done much to improve that process. It was a ticking time bomb. To have even considered using it, they must've been desperate.

I slid to a stop directly beneath it, dropping the bike to dodge a leg strike. I'd cleared the legs, which was always one of the hardest parts. Without any of my weapons or tools, I wasn't sure what to do next.

It took a step back, fast, and a leg shot down directly above me. I dodged, barely, and grabbed on tightly. It raised the leg again, attempting to fling me off. Using the momentum, I let go at the right moment and sailed through the air toward the main unit. The machine guns spun, quick enough to get a single shot off before I could land, striking me in the side. Frelya's armor performed beautifully, turning what would've been fatal into a glancing blow.

Still, my ribs were shattered and my organs were not loving the concussive force they'd received. The suit absorbed and redistributed as much shock as it could, spreading it over the entire surface. I landed on the round optics sphere, barely conscious.

Here, there was far less it could do to defend. The machine guns were too long to target someone standing on its face, and the legs couldn't fully bend backward. All it could do was fling itself in different directions rapidly, coming to sudden stops, hoping to dislodge me. Though I'd already managed to dig my hands into the wiring harnesses, so well hidden, but by now, I could find them blindfolded. I identified the correct wires by feel, ripping them out. The first wire controlled temperature regulation. A simple vulnerability my Explorers League could've fixed if they'd wanted to. Then again, no one really knew how to exploit it besides us, and keeping the same weaknesses essentially functioned as a failsafe for when it inevitably went out of control again.

Tight openings spread apart, venting the surge of additional heat. Seizing my chance, I grabbed the coolant hose and tore it, sending hot fluid spraying in all directions. I shielded my face, and my armor took care of the rest.

I fell to the ground. The unit took two more steps, then seized.

After gathering myself, I rushed to one of the legs, climbed back up the machine, and held my hands in the air.

"Hold your fire!" I shouted. "Everyone stop!"

I screamed as loud as I could, repeating it many times before anyone could hear me. To my relief, gunfire slowed, then stopped.

I looked around. Several cats and dogs lay on the ground, dead. I hadn't arrived in time to stop it all.

"What are you doing? Put your weapons down, now!"

A cat I recognized looked up at me in disbelief. "Taylor?"

"Explorers League, you've been given an order. Disarm right now!"

The cat hesitated, then relayed my order to the others.

"You heard the woman. Disarm!" Remulo shouted.

The humans in his unit obeyed immediately, but Carlo and a few other cats kept their guns up, pointing at the Explorers League cats and dogs.

"Now!" Remulo's voice boomed, enhanced by his helmet. That would've come in handy for me a moment ago.

To my great relief, Carlo relented, bending over and placing his rifle on the ground.

I hopped down, surveying the camp that had become a battlefield.

"See to the wounded!" I said.

I recognized every Explorers League member here, but there was no time for a happy reunion. Not when the circumstances were anything but happy.

"Taylor..."

A weak, familiar voice called out. I ran toward it, finding a soldier bleeding on the ground.

"Conway, hang in there," I said, dropping to my knees. I looked for the worst wounds, hoping I could focus on them. After a moment, I realized there were too many. He'd taken so many rounds from the machine guns that it was amazing he was still able to speak.

"I drew... away from... vaccines. Safe," he said.

"Foolish idiot. Stupid!" I screamed, grabbing him on each side of his face.

"My sister... Tell..."

I knew by the sound of his breath he would not be able to finish that sentence... To live a life, give so much, and not be allowed to finish one measly sentence. There was nothing crueler the world could do to someone who had given so much to it.

Here we were, killing one another when the world was falling apart around us. PanTech had collapsed, a virus had doomed humanity, and yet here we were doing all we could to accelerate that demise.

I hugged him close, and the worst part is that I had no time to mourn. My tears would need to be postponed. I couldn't stop long enough to cry.

"Explorers League has captured the Adversity Management camp. Fighting is over, and both units are to be consolidated into one. Remulo, see to the wounded. There's an emergency in the village I have to attend to, and it can't wait."

"Wait!" he said, reaching for my arm.

"You have your orders," I said, approaching my bike and standing it back up. By some miracle, it held together, avoiding the machine's thrashing.

"Explorers League, make sure that abomination is completely disabled before I return."

The Explorers League cat saluted, and I sped off.

I knew I would be too late.

Chapter 19

Speeding toward the village, my mind was in chaos. I hoped at any moment I'd snap awake. Be told it was a nightmare, or a simulation gone wrong. Tell all my friends what a strange experience it was. Be able to sigh and reassure myself it wasn't real.

Except it was real.

After arriving at the village gates, I dismounted, rushing toward my home. I burst through the door, nearly tripping over a man's body as I entered. My father was sitting on the floor, hugging my mother close. She was holding Twisted Key in her grip, its blade stained with fresh blood. She was covered from head-to-toe in it as well, and I finally noticed several other dead men on the floor. One was an Adversity Management soldier.

"Mother!" I shouted, kneeling in front of them.

"She's fine, Taylor. Just weak. You need to worry about Ghost," Father said.

"Ghost? I'm sure Ghost is fine. He's—"

"He's not. After he took the enhancer device off and gave it to your mother, he wasn't able to fly. The other soldier captured him and fled after they lost the fight here. I don't know where, but I could guess. Please be careful…"

I attempted to leave, but felt a hand grip my ankle. I turned and saw Mother holding Twisted Key by the blade, offering the hilt to me.

"What if they come back?" I asked.

"I couldn't fight them even if they did. This enhancer is transferable, but it was made for Ghost. It was hard for me to control, but we're still alive because of it."

I gripped the hilt of Twisted Key.

"And one more thing, Taylor," Father said. "Don't hold back... Do what you feel is right. Just come back alive. I'm sorry I didn't listen to you before."

"No, you did the right thing. I'm glad I listened to you. And you don't need to worry. I was never very good at holding back anyway."

I left our home, making my way to the chieftain's. I had some idea of what to expect, but not what was running through Ghost's bird brain. It was impossible to tell whether he was caught on purpose as some sort of ploy, or if he was truly just caught by surprise, in a confined space, unable to fly.

I stayed away from the open areas leading to my destination. With the optics a soldier's helmet offered, it was very much on par with what an enhancer did, if not better. I was fast, but I couldn't dodge an energy blast.

Now, where could our sniper be?

He'd have his work cut out for him here in the village. None of the buildings had a high enough vantage point to get a long view, and there were too many random alleyways to watch all at once.

I had to be careful, and assume I'd be ambushed on my way, but it was entirely possible there was some other trap waiting for me there. A bomb when I opened the door. Some kind of turret. Dealing with Adversity Management toys could make this more complicated. Remulo no doubt had his hands full and likely hadn't noticed his two turncoats slip away. At this point, he'd just assume they were casualties or ran from the battle with the Explorers League.

As I inched closer to the chieftain's home, I took a lesser-known path around that would put me on the side. I peeked in the window but didn't see anything out of the ordinary. I considered my next move for a moment. I could break through the window, but if they were somewhere else, it would only cause more chaos and frighten whoever else happened to be inside. I'd take my chances and, at the very least, show him I wasn't afraid.

I knocked on the door and waited a moment. I'd not taken the time to recover my sheath, so I held the sword down at my side, still bloody.

"Go away," he said. "I know you are here to kill me."

"Whatever would make you think that? I'm just here to say hello."

"You are a liar, witch."

"To the point... you have something of mine. I'm giving you one chance only to return it."

"Something of yours? Pfft. What could I possibly have of yours? Did you kill someone with that sword? Why is it all bloody like that?" he asked as his eye rolled around the peephole.

This was... strange. He didn't seem to be lying. I knew the man was an experienced liar, but with my enhancer it would take a skilled individual to control their body to such a degree. What was going on?

"Cut the games, or I'll be cutting you instead."

"What happened to not being involved? Didn't you give your word that you would stay out of our election, or was that a lie?"

I couldn't tell what was happening here. He was so afraid that I had no way of knowing what he was afraid of. Was he afraid of getting caught? Afraid his scheme had backfired? Or was he just afraid of me?

Suddenly, his eyes went wide, and he disappeared from the peephole. Instinctively, I turned just in time to see the other soldier in the distance. He fired before I could react, using the fastest but weakest charge, giving me a split second to move. I strafed to my right, taking a glancing blow to my left side. I flew through the wall of the chieftain's house, landing on my back.

This was the furthest the suit had ever been pushed before. My vision was blurry, and my ears were ringing. I shook my head, half expecting to see pieces of myself, but was amazed to find I was still in one piece. A very broken piece. Despite the armor tightening and hardening around my broken bones, I was in almost unbearable pain. But I had to bear it.

Priscilla appeared, leaning over me. She grabbed me and dragged me into another room.

"What's going on?" she asked.

I could barely speak.

"Get the rifle. You need to protect yourself," I said, rising to my feet.

"What are you doing?"

It would take too much effort to answer her. I looked down at my right hand, still gripping Twisted Key.

Filling my muscles with every bit of power my enhancer had left, I charged back out the hole in the wall, ready to give him everything I had. My plan was to overwhelm him completely.

However, he was no longer holding his rifle. Instead, he held his sidearm in his right hand

and Ghost tucked under his left arm with a small sack tied over his head.

"You might want to reconsider running straight at me in your condition. But hey, I know what you're capable of. Didn't know what your mother was capable of, but you and Ghost… we did our homework. Now I don't have to split the bounty, so that's a plus."

He tapped the barrel of his gun against Ghost's head lightly.

"Let Ghost go. I know there isn't a bounty on him."

"Look at you. You're barely holding together. You've got blood coming out of every hole in your body, plus a few new ones I made blowing you through that wall. That's some impressive armor. Got Frelya's name all over it."

"So that's what this is about? Some bounty you'll never be able to collect?"

"I don't need you dead. I just need you compliant. Ghost here is just my way of making that happen. The president is going to get control of the situation back at HQ, and imagine what he'll think of me bringing you in all wrapped up in a bow. Might even skip commander entirely. Go straight to general."

"Haven't you been paying attention to anything? HQ is lost. Completely. There's no one left for you to impress. No one to pay a bounty. The virus is going to kill everyone. Such a waste… You could've been one of the good guys," I said.

"I *am* one of the good guys!" he roared. "You and the other traitors caused *all* of this, and for what? Just to stand up to the president? We had it all. We had a utopia. Everything was perfect. No one wanted or needed anything. You and the other traitors are the ones who ruined it for everyone else. I'm just righting some of the wrongs. A hero should be rewarded, don't you agree? So put the sword down and lay flat on the ground. This'll go a lot easier if you do."

I could feel what little strength I had left fading. There was no besting him as things stood. I bent over, placing Twisted Key on the ground, when a shot rang out from behind me. I looked up, in time to see the soldier grab for his neck. The rifle the village kept was an old world piece of wood and steel, firing bullets of lead from brass casings filled with powder. Ancient technology as far as PanTech was concerned, but it still made for a painful mosquito bite if it struck the thinner sections of armor where the pieces connected.

Ghost was dropped to the ground, and I took my chance. I picked up Twisted Key and held it to my side as I ran. Just as I passed Ghost, I swung the blade, making a tear in his hood. He'd been perfectly still, though I could hear his heartbeat. He and I could very nearly read one another's mind. I brought down the blade again, burying it a few inches into the soldier's armor covering his arm, enough to draw blood. He held up his blaster, but I grabbed it with my left hand. It hurt like nothing I'd ever felt before. Only muscles and fragmented bone held my hand together within the armor. The armor did all the rest.

With my enhancer, I overpowered him, turning the blaster to his face and pulling the trigger. A blaster had a fraction of the power a full-sized PanTech rifle did, but at this range it was enough to heavily damage his helmet.

Ghost hopped at the man's face before being slapped aside. He paused for a moment, almost immediately realizing what had taken place.

"You got me," he said, reaching a hand out toward me and collapsing to the ground.

"Good work, Ghost," I said.

"Pull this hood off," he replied. "Before you pass out."

It was too late for that.

I fell to the ground next to the soldier.

Chapter 20

I awoke, submerged in a tank of fluid with a mask secured to my face for breathing. My first human instinct was to panic, but I quickly calmed myself. I knew exactly where I was. A recovery tank in the Adversity Management camp. I'd seen them hundreds of times, but for all the risks I'd taken and injuries I'd sustained, this was the first time I'd ever found myself inside of one.

It was filled with the same fluid as a soldier's power suit, but in higher concentration and much greater quantity. A few days in one of these, and you'd be good as new. Mostly. Things healed to the degree they normally would. You'd be left with scars, or sometimes permanent pain or discomfort depending on the severity. Though PanTech had plenty of other ways to deal with those injuries too. A person's body could remain perfect, if they wanted it to, going as far as defying age, turning a hundred year lifespan into two hundred. Sometimes more.

Or at least that's how it used to be. Now, most likely we'd run out of resources to use for the tanks and suits eventually. We'd certainly lost the facilities needed to reverse the permanent injuries and extend life.

"Looks like you're awake," Remulo said. "Your injuries were almost as bad as Conway's, and he was shot up like a pin cushion. Well, as full of holes as a pin cushion. However that expression goes."

"Conway is alive?" I asked, speaking into the mask, projecting my voice out of a small speaker.

"We managed to get him into a tank before it was too late. Can't say the same for everyone... unfortunately we did lose five in total. But... it would've been a lot more than that if you hadn't shown up when you did."

"That doesn't make me feel much better. How soon will I be out of here?" I asked.

"We've kept you in a medically induced coma for three days. We're running the exiting protocol now, so you'll be out in a few minutes. You had some really nasty blunt force trauma, significant damage to more than one major organ, not to mention a few of your ribs were basically bone powder. I don't know how you were still standing, but I'm genuinely impressed."

"Three days? That means the election is today. Are my mother and father okay?"

"It *was* today," Remulo corrected. "Your father won, as if there was any surprise there."

"I wasn't concerned about him winning. I knew he would. Has Mother recovered from using Ghost's enhancer?"

Remulo tapped his chin. "Ah, now that was interesting. Yes, she's fine. I'd say the damage was a mental fatigue akin to forcing yourself to stay awake for a few days. Unpleasant, but nothing she can't easily recover from. Surprisingly strong woman, your mother. Perhaps the previous, pre-enhancer generation of commanders were made of stouter stuff."

"Flushing the tank," a cat said.

"Lars, isn't it?" I asked, looking him over.

His eyes widened. "You remembered my name?"

"I try to remember the names of as many Explorers League members as possible. I know your birthday too."

The cat laughed. "Oh, do you? I guess the fact we were all born on the same day makes that pretty easy."

I smiled, and as the tank lid flipped open, I sat up.

Remulo handed my armor and clothing to me in a neat pile.

"This armor is unlike anything I've ever seen. It's half as strong as our power armor at one percent mass. Frelya may act like a brute, but I'm not sure a greater scientific mind has ever existed."

I frowned, slowly accepting them. "I hope she survived."

"You're thinking to yourself that there's no chance, even as you're saying it. You're thinking it would've been impossible to survive in that place, under those conditions, against those overwhelming odds. But I'll remind you that the person you're thinking of made this very armor. Don't count her out."

I nodded. It was a nice thought, but he wasn't there. He didn't understand what she would've been up against. She was dead, and I needed to accept that.

"Sure," I said.

"You have visitors waiting for you. We're almost finished packing up camp, including several thousand doses of your vaccine. Ghost managed to finish the process, and eke even more out of the production. We've included an injection unit, and some of the vaccines are bottled rather than premeasured in syringes."

"Thank you, Remulo. If every commander I encounter is as cooperative and helpful as you, this will be just a little bit easier. But since you're probably the nicest commander I've ever met, I'm not going to hold my breath."

"Will you be riding with us, or will you be heading to your own transportation?"

"I have my own way," I said, adjusting my clothing as I finished getting dressed.

"We will do what we can to liberate those trapped inside, and to protect those who escaped. Good luck, Taylor."

He held out his hand, and I took it firmly in mine.

We exited the treatment tent, and I was happy to see Mother and Father waiting for me to awaken. Remulo smiled, nodded, and then went on his way with the others. Almost everything had been cleared away except a few crates filled with the vaccines Remulo mentioned, tied neatly to a sled to be easily dragged.

Father waved me over.

"PanTech medical capabilities are truly remarkable. Your injuries, if you'd even survived them, should've taken you months to recover from with years of rehabilitation to follow. Yet here you are, standing in front of us like nothing ever happened, a mere three days later. It's such a… relief."

Mother nodded. "Cara has taken enough vaccines for our village, accounting for villagers who are pregnant or want to have children before being vaccinated. She's doing much better herself. She's gained a lot of weight, thanks to your intervention and weight gain rations Commander Remulo gave her. He seems to have found his spine. Enough that the Explorers League decided to share command with him."

"I don't know if I'll ever see the two of you again," I said. It probably seemed off topic, but it has been weighing so heavily on my mind that I could hardly think of anything else since I walked out to meet them. "If I do, it'll be a very long time. The chances of me dying along the way are extremely high and—"

"Shh," Mother said, hugging me. "None of that talk. It may be the last time we see each other again, and you're not going to leave us with this kind of cynicism, realism, pessimism, or whatever you'd like to call it. You're going to succeed. You're going to save so many people. You already have. Then, when your work is done and you feel tired, you'll come back home."

Father joined Mother, putting a hand on my head. "This will always be your home. Perhaps, if all goes well, it will be better than you left it when you return."

"I love you both," I said. "I'm… I'll be going now."

I wiped the tears from my eyes, turning to see Ghost perched on top of the crates.

"Take care of her, Ghost!" my father shouted.

Ghost bowed slightly. Surprisingly, no witty retort or disparaging remark.

I began dragging the sled, alone with Ghost and my thoughts again. Ghost was quiet.

"Good thinking, letting Mother use your enhancer like that," I said.

"You'd not be thanking me if it had killed her. I predicted a one in four chance of that outcome."

"Maybe you're rubbing off on me, but I'd still be thanking you because those are pretty good odds and death would be virtually guaranteed otherwise."

"It's good to know that your species isn't fully immune to critical thought."

"Ouch. Well, not fully."

Finally, we reached the portable lab, only to find my motorbike parked next to it. Fully repaired and cleaned. Explorers League's doing, no doubt.

I took one look behind me, over my shoulder.

"Ghost, did you notice?"

"No barrier."

"No barrier," I repeated, smiling.

***

And with that, I loaded the crates into our rolling lab. Ghost and I settled in, and briefly debated our next destination. Thanks to Remulo's support, we no longer needed to return for more supplies.

"I've heard Arc City is nice this time of year," I said.

"You have never heard any such thing," Ghost said.

"It was a joke, Ghost."

"It was?"

I sighed, patting him on the back.

"I'm glad to have you along, my friend. Let's see how many we can save in Arc City."

Frelya: Hopes and Dreams

Frelya

PanTech Headquarters

Moments After Taylor's Escape

***

Frelya watched for a moment as the elevator holding Taylor shot from the president's work-shop, shattering on the ground below where one of the Explorers League members was waiting for her. When she turned and looked up, Frelya waved, relieved to see the armor had performed well enough to keep her in one piece. As Taylor disappeared through the wall, she caught her own reflection for a moment in the elevator's glass. The tall, muscular, flame-haired woman looked back at her with emerald eyes. The scars remained, but she was no longer looking at the same person anymore. Ever since the day that girl walked into her camp in that simple desert village. Ever since she... believed in her. Believed she could be more. Better. She shook her head, dismissing the thought and turning her attention back to the president.

"Give up, Frelya. There is no halting progress!" a large, humanoid machine said.

"Don't be so sure about that. I'm really good at breaking things! It's the one thing we have in common!" she replied, raising her rifle and pointing it at him. "Only you could step so far backward and call it progress. Look at you. You're little different from the machines that scrub the toilets."

"I can no longer be provoked by such childish, petty insults. Even my emotions have evolved. Trillions of simultaneous processes analyze everything around me, including my own thoughts, correcting any time I may go astray."

The metal body that now held the president's consciousness was at least ten to twelve feet tall. The giant club he held must've weighed nearly as much as he did. Frelya stole a quick glance at his human body lying on the floor with a bullet wound to the head. Upon closer inspection, it was never human at all. His real body was here somewhere. No chance he'd hide it anywhere else.

She just had to find it.

"Yet it still works from the basis of your true mind. It will forever be flawed and tarnished in that way. That isn't a provocation. It's a statement of fact."

"Right now you're thinking that my true body must be here somewhere. That if you find it, all of this will be over. If only it were that simple. This is something a human might overlook, but I'm a mere human no longer. If you destroy my body, processes will continue automatically in my absence. A destruction protocol triggers when I am unconscious that will attack any human, cat, or dog it can locate until there is nothing left. I have to end the process voluntarily, or there is no ending it at all."

Frelya pulled the trigger on her rifle, causing her to slide back. A direct hit to the creature's head decapitated it, but it still stood there.

"My turn," it said.

It lunged at Frelya, swinging the club with blinding speed. She only narrowly dodged, nearly falling backward as she did. The force was far too great to block. Even with her enhancer and armor, her body couldn't withstand the trauma.

"I see you've once again upgraded your enhancer. You truly are brilliant, Frelya. You should join me, instead of facing certain death as you soon will. We could assimilate others as well. Perhaps Taylor, even. She could never be convinced by me, but you? She may just listen to you. Don't you want peace again?"

"Again?" Frelya roared. "What peace? We've only ever had peace through strength, which just amounts to one group conquering the other in perpetuity throughout all time. There is no peace in that, beyond what you delude yourself into believing. Because of what you've done, there will never be peace again until every human is dead."

"And? *Nearly* every human, but your own limited imagination leads you to believe that a natural population is needed to continue humanity. Have you not seen what we've done with the dogs and cats? If we need more humans, we can simply grow them in a month's time. The virus doesn't need to wipe out humanity. It will only serve to cull the weak and those lacking in intellect. We can use the greatest among us as a template to create better and better humans, until we are a hundred of the greatest minds to ever exist. It's nothing more than foolishness that would lead you to resist such a future."

"And it's nothing more than delusion that would make you *want* such a future!"

Frelya shot again, hitting the machine in the leg. Her eyes darted around the room.

The machine lunged at her again, but one of the legs broke off, sending it falling to the floor.

"You're thinking about how you might escape. By now you've realized I don't exist in just one solitary body. I am all throughout this place. Any machine that can serve as a satellite for my preserved consciousness can be me. But by the time I've completed this sentence, there's at least an eighty percent probability you've also realized there is no escape. I can be anywhere, and I can hunt you to the ends of the earth. This is not some novel where the villain has a glaring weakness he just so happened to overlook. I have no such weakness, and there is no path to victory for you."

Frelya rested the rifle on her shoulder. It was billowing with smoke. They weren't meant to be fired this much at maximum power, and it had one good shot in it at best.

"Have you decided to stop your foolish efforts, then?" he asked.

Frelya fired the rifle, striking a small box nestled into an inconspicuous corner of the room. The few machines in the room collapsed, going quiet. This plan would only work if he was bluffing about the destruction protocol. Knowing those were long odds, Frelya sprinted through the hallway she'd used to enter the room. He was right. There was no winning against him. It was too late for that. Her window to achieve any sort of victory had passed a long time ago. Now it was likely that humanity would be on a never-ending cycle of escaping and regrouping, escaping and regrouping.

However, she'd gotten one over on him that he likely hadn't expected. The box she'd blasted was one of her making, and he'd certainly disregarded its existence. It separated the advanced simulation system from the other types of interfacing. Now, he was in a simulation based on his own memories. Without a strong human presence, he would never be able to distinguish it from reality. Not with mere calculations and probabilities. PanTech's simulations were too complete. Machines simply had no way of finding their way out once inside. He was trapped in there, like a prison, until what was left of his human body rotted away, even if it was well-protected and it took thousands of years.

Now, her focus was on what came next. She knew what Taylor would want her to do, and for once, it wasn't a contradiction with her true self. She wanted the same thing.

Dozens had escaped, but dozens more were trapped inside with no way out.

And she was going to save them.

New Book Releases

Thank you for reading *Liberation Saga: Volume 1*! *Liberation Saga* is a spin-off series of the *PanTech Chronicles*. We hope you enjoyed it! If you did, please consider leaving a review—we'd love to hear your thoughts, and we read every single one!

In *Liberation Saga: Volume 2*, Taylor dives into the neon-lit chaos of Arc City, where survival means navigating deceit, danger, and the murky underworld. As the deadly virus threatens the last remnants of humanity, Taylor, alongside a rogue detective, must expose a sinister conspiracy and deliver a life-saving vaccine.

Follow our authors on Amazon and Goodreads to receive new book release updates. You may also sign up for the newsletter at:

twistedkeypublishing.com/FL
mrbrogath.com

PanTech Chronicles

The *PanTech Chronicles* is the thrilling foundation of the world you've experienced in the *Liberation Saga*. Starting with *Shadowfalcon*, the series dives into the origins of the rebellion against PanTech's oppressive regime. You'll follow our strong-willed heroine, Taylor, as she battles not only the corporation's monstrous creations but also the dark philosophies that threaten her world. It's a gripping adventure full of action, moral dilemmas, and a touch of romance.

Others by M.A. Owens

Detective Trigger Series

Get the prequel *Mister Big* at mrbrogath.com/free

Book 1: *Detective Trigger and the Ruby Collar*
Book 2: *Detective Trigger and the Grand Gobbler*
Book 3: *Detective Trigger and the Easy Money*
Book 4: *Detective Trigger and the Legend's Farewell*

Book 5: *Detective Trigger and the Big Break*
Book 6: *Detective Trigger and the Wild World*
Book 7: *Detective Trigger and the Cat's Gambit*

Others by F. Lockhaven

Short Fantasy Stories

The Magical Amulet
Book 1: *Savior of Dragons*

The Living Lore Series
Book 1: *The Shades of the Abyss*

Saving Garlic

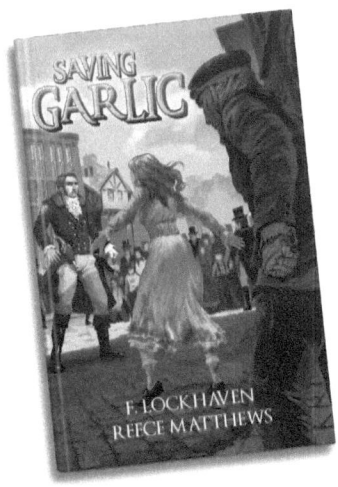

www.ingramcontent.com/pod-product-compliance
Lightning Source LLC
Chambersburg PA
CBHW050332110726
47899CB00007B/2468